The Dopefiend:

Part 2 of the Dopeman's Trilogy

The Dopefiend:

Part 2 of the Dopeman's Trilogy

JaQuavis Coleman

www.urbanbooks.net

Urban Books, LLC
97 N18th Street
Wyandanch NY, 11798

The Dopefiend: Part 2 of the Dopeman's Trilogy
© Copyright 2010 JaQuavis Coleman

ISBN 13: 978-1-60162-629-5
ISBN 10: 1-60162-629-0

First Mass Market Printing October 2014
First Printing May 2010
Printed in the United States of America

10 9 8

*This is a work of fiction. Any references or similari-
ties to actual events, real people, living, or dead, or
to real locales are intended to give the novel a sense
of reality. Any similarity in other names, charac-
ters, places, and incidents is entirely coincidental.*

Distributed by Kensington Publishing Corp.
Submit Wholesale Orders to:
Kensington Publishing Corp.
C/O Penguin Group(USA) Inc.
Attention: Order Processing
405 Murray Hill Parkway
East Rutherford, NJ 07073-2316
Phone: 1-800-526-0275
Fax: 1-800-227-9604

In Loving Memory of
Lovie L. Price

Preface

On December 24, 2009, Hazel Brown jumped off the New York Bridge at exactly 11:51 p.m., and her body was never found. Legend has . . . the river underneath the bridge has no bottom and holds many secrets and shames. Many people alleged, that by jumping, it was her way to escape her life's ills that this cold world had to offer. People who knew her well also said that she is in a much happier place now. A place where there is no more deceit, no more pain, no more drugs, and no more heartbreak. When you read this story, know that I put my all into this novel in an effort to tell the story of a young woman, who by the time she was eighteen, had seen more than most wise men could ever fathom. Through these pages I give you the raw, untold account of a fascinating lady who I once knew . . . who I once loved . . . who I once hated. Please read in between the lines carefully and walk with her as her story allows you to look through the eyes of a young black girl lost and a stone-cold dopefiend. Hazel Brown is a person who we all know . . . a person who somehow got lost in the sauce and fell victim to the flipside of the drug game. Hazel's character symbolizes something so much bigger than herself. There is a whole nation full of young, black women just like her. No lengthy acknowledgements were needed for this book . . . this one is for the Hazels of the world. This is her true story.

JaQuavis Coleman

Prologue

The night's chilled wind blew through the young woman's hair as the full moon provided illumination, giving the entire park a blue hue. The girl's name was Hazel, Hazel Brown to be exact. She walked aimlessly through the park in a total daze, with a big smile on her face, feeling like the queen of the night. She wore a glamorous and expensive, all-white mink coat that hung over her shoulders. The cold air from the winter's chill hit Hazel's face like a ton of bricks; making her slightly cringe. She quickly dipped her head inside of her coat, covering the bottom half of her face to avoid "the hawk" also known as winter in mid-December. Hazel headed to the bridge and took a deep breath as she glanced over the edge and saw the long drop into the water. She blocked out all noise and the only thing she could hear was the sound of the water that was beneath her. The sound of the waves dancing on top of the large pallet of water was scintillating to the human ears. It sounded so peaceful, so serene to Hazel's ears. She slowly kicked off her stilettos and carefully climbed onto the ledge as she tried to keep her balance. The cold rail that she stood on sent chills up her body as the frost pressed against the bottom of her feet. She cautiously balanced herself on the ledge as she tried her best to not let the slippery, icy rails get the best of her. She then pulled off her bloody mink and released it into the water, exposing her thousand-dollar black dress made by Hazel's favorite Italian designer. She looked down at the gorgeous view and watched as the moon's light bounced off of the small waves. She then looked back at Apple who stood a few yards away from her tipping the mime who had just put on a brief show for them. He was so busy admiring the mime's precise movements, he didn't even notice Hazel slip away and prepare to do the unthinkable.

Hazel began to reflect on her life and it seemed like her entire twenty-two years on Earth had flashed before her eyes. Hazel balanced herself until she was steady and opened her arms as if she were a soaring eagle in the free skies. She looked over at her forearm and saw the needle marks that would forever leave scars on her skin. It reminded her of her journey and all that she had been through over the years. She smiled and then closed her eyes, feeling liberated as a bird. She inhaled deeply, smiled, and then without hesitation she let her body fall forward. . . .

Chapter One

One Year Earlier in Flint, MI

"Yo, when I catch you . . . I'm going to kill you. I put that on everything," Rico whispered under his breath as he stood completely naked with both of his hands up. His head was cocked to the side as Millie held a blood-filled syringe to the side of his neck, almost piercing his skin. Rico was being held up in the backroom of a dope house and he couldn't believe what was happening; he had just got caught slipping. He clenched his jaws as tightly as he could, displaying his anger as the veins formed in his temples. Millie, on the other hand, was smiling as she thought about how her plan had worked perfectly. She had caught Rico slipping and now the only thing on her mind was shooting some of Rico's good smack into her veins. Millie was almost twice his age and had outwitted him. Rico's young sixteen-year-old mind fell for the okey-doke.

"Yeah, yeah. Save all that talking for somebody else. Hazel, check in his back pockets too,"

Millie instructed as she watched Hazel rummage through Rico's pants that were sprawled out on the floor along with his other clothing.

"I can't believe this shit," Rico spat angrily as he rolled his eyes and hated himself for being so naïve to Millie's game. What he thought was going to be a ménage à trois with a couple of dopefiends, ended up being a robbery. He watched as Hazel nervously looked through his pants and coat pockets searching for his bundles of heroin. Hazel continued to search frantically while frequently peeking at Rico to make sure Millie had him under control. Millie had Rico in a chokehold and wished that Hazel would hurry up, because she was growing more nervous by the second. Millie told Rico that the syringe was filled with her AIDS-infected blood, but that was far from the truth. Well, at least Millie hoped that she didn't have the deadly disease.

"Got it!" Hazel yelled as she held up the small bundles of heroin that were inside the inside pocket of Rico's down coat. She held the dope up in the air as if she had found a hidden treasure. Hazel also grabbed the wad of money that Rico had in his pockets and quickly stood up. Hazel stuffed the money and dope in her bra and headed for the back window. Before she reached the window she saw Rico's gun on the dresser and she grabbed that too.

"You got everything?" Millie asked as she shook nervously while still having a firm grasp on Rico. He only stood five feet four inches and weighed a buck thirty at the most, so Millie was in complete control.

"Yeah, I got it. Let's go!" Hazel said as she put one foot out of the window and sat on the window-pane with half of her body inside of the house, waiting for Millie.

"Hurry, pass me that gun," Millie ordered as she held out one hand so that she could get it. Hazel placed the gun in Millie's hand and could barely place it in her palm because she was shaking so badly. Millie finally got the gun and took the syringe from Rico's neck. She then pointed his own gun at him. She slowly walked backward until she reached the window. Rico just watched her as he kept both of his hands up and watched them escape. He had a small grin on his face as he thought about how he would kill both of them when he caught up with them.

Millie quickly jumped out the window along with Hazel and they took off running full speed down Wood Street. The sounds of their feet crunching the snow and their heavy breathing were the only sounds at the early hour. They tried their best not to slip on the icy streets as they hauled ass. They heard the voice of Rico yelling as they cut through houses and finally got out of earshot from him. They dipped into a low-key spot that they had used a couple times before. It was a boarded-up house that only a few other fiends knew about. For some odd reason, the electricity and the water were still on in the house, which only worked as a plus for them. It was their warm, secret get-high spot.

They came in through the back door and without even catching their breath they both headed to the small, dusty table that sat in the middle of the floor. They both took a seat in the old wooden chairs as Hazel reached into her bra and pulled out the dope. Millie quickly sat the gun down that they had gotten from Rico and rubbed her hands together, knowing she was about to get a treat. Millie's eyes lit up as she began to feel the tingling sensation in her arms, pure anticipation for the good smack that she was about to inject into her body. Both of their stomachs were bubbling and agonizing pains shot through them as their bodies craved the drug. Millie had even caught the runs earlier that morning, jonesin' for the drug. Hazel gripped her stomach and slightly bent over trying to get the pain to subside. "Hurry, Millie," Hazel begged.

Millie grabbed the spoon that was on the table along with the dope. She poured the dope into the spoon and the strong odor from the heroin filled the air and only made them more impatient. The smell slightly resembled vinegar and it was like heaven for their noses. Hazel watched closely as Millie set them up. Hazel never "set-up," she always let Millie do it. Millie was ten years Hazel's senior and had had much more experience than her, so it made sense.

"You smell that? This that *Lady Luck* right here," Millie bragged as she gently thumped the baggy. *Lady Luck* was the latest, top-of-the-line heroin in the hood. "Rico always got that good shit on deck," Millie stated as she never took her eyes off the dope and smiled in awe, similar to a small child. She opened a second pack and poured that into the spoon also. She then gave Hazel a bottle cap.

"Go put some water in that, Hazelnut," Millie said, calling Hazel by a nickname she had given her when she was younger. Hazel snapped out of her daze, grabbed the cap, and quickly headed to the kitchen to put some water in it. She quickly returned and Millie pulled a syringe out of her pocket and soaked up the water through the needle. She quickly squirted a small amount in the spoon. She then raised the spoon up, while Hazel held a flame underneath it. They both watched as the drug melted into the water and began to bubble. Both of their hearts began to race as they were about to get their breakfast, a.k.a. the first shot of the day. Once the contents were fully melted, Hazel quickly grabbed the belt that was on the table and wrapped it around her right arm. She tightened the belt around her arm and placed the leather in her mouth to maintain the tightness while also freeing her left hand. Hazel began to smack her forearm with two fingers repeatedly, desperately searching for a vein. A big, green vein finally began to form in Hazel's forearm and she smiled as the belt was held secure in between her teeth.

"It's too hot. You gotta wait," Millie said as she held the spoon up and slowly shook it.

"Fuck that. I'm good. Let me hit that," Hazel pleaded as she pulled out her own syringe and placed it in the spoon. She sucked up the heroin and immediately placed the needle to the bulging vein that had formed in her forearm. The sizzling sound of the metal touching her skin sounded and her skin began to blister, but Hazel didn't care that she was burning herself. She just wanted to feel the "magic" of the drug. Hazel slowly injected the smack into her veins and her body became limp as her eyes rolled in the back of her head. It seemed as if she was having a sexual orgasm by her body movements, but it was the euphoric effect that heroin had on a woman. Hazel began to nod off and Millie quickly took the belt from around Hazel's arm so that she could get her fix.

"This shit is . . ." Hazel mumbled, but before she could even tell Millie how good it was, she nodded off completely.

Chapter Two

Smack! Smack!

Millie was about to smack Hazel across the face for a third time, but Hazel opened her eyes just as she raised her hand. "Wake up, Hazel! Rico is outside looking for us!" Millie said as she grabbed up Hazel by the collar and sat her upright. Hazel had been slumped down in the chair for the last thirty minutes, nodding.

"Wha . . . What?" Hazel asked in confusion as her eyes shot wide open and looked around. She had to snap back to reality, not remembering where she was at for a moment.

"Let's go out the back. He is outside asking people questions," Millie said nervously as she scrambled to get the needles off the table. Millie then walked over to the front door and looked out the peephole. She saw Rico's motorcycle parked on the curb. He was talking to another junkie and the junkie pointed at the house that they were currently in, tipping Rico off. Rico pulled out a gun and walked toward the house.

"Oh, shit! Let's get the fuck out of here!" Mille ordered in an exasperated whisper as she grabbed the gun and dope, stuffing them into her oversized purse. Hazel quickly jumped up and they headed toward the back door. Just as they reached the back door, they heard Rico kicking in the front one.

"I'ma blow yo' head off," Rico yelled as he saw them fleeing out of the back of the house. Millie and Hazel darted out the back of the house and into the backyard. Rico was coming through the house ready to blast. Not only did they hit his pockets by robbing him, but they also bruised his ego, which brought out the worst in a man. He was furious.

"Come on, Hazel," Millie urged as she climbed and hopped over the fence like an Olympic athlete. Although Millie was in her early thirties, she moved like a youngster, especially while she was being chased. Once Millie cleared the fence, Hazel tried to climb it, but her high was still peaking and it was causing her to move slower than usual. She struggled up the fence and Millie was on the ground hurrying her.

"Come on, Hazelnut! Get yo' ass over that damn fence," she hissed. As Hazel tried to hop over, a loud gun blast erupted and Hazel could hear the bullet whiz past her shoulder.

"Bitch, I'ma kill you," Rico said as he held the smoking gun in his hand. He aimed and prepared to fire again, but it was too late because Hazel had cleared the fence.

As soon as Hazel's feet hit the ground, they both took off. Hazel and Millie ran full speed down Avenue B, trying to get as far away from Rico as possible. They cut through some yards and hopped a couple more fences as they sprinted until they ran out of breath.

"You think we lost him?" Hazel asked eagerly as they both rested their hands on their knees and leaned against the brick wall of Dort Elementary School.

"Yeah, we shook him," Millie said as she rested her hand on her chest. "I'm getting too old for this shit."

"You okay?" Hazel asked as she looked at Millie who was having a hard time breathing.

"Yeah, I'm good," Millie responded. Hazel looked at Millie, the only female who she had ever trusted. In fact, Millie was more like a mother figure to Hazel, always having her back and was the only family she had left. Although Millie was a dopefiend, Hazel looked up to her. Matter of fact, Millie was the one who introduced the drug to Hazel at the tender age of sixteen. That was something that Millie painfully regretted every day.

"Let's catch a cab home," Millie said as she began to walk toward the main road called North Saginaw Street. Hazel followed closely as they made their way onto the main street trying to flag down a cab.

"One of these mufuckas better stop, shit!" Millie said as she reached into her bra and pulled out a box of Newport cigarettes. She put one in her mouth and it dangled from the right side of her mouth as she squinted one of her eyes and she lit it up. She took a deep pull and tapped her foot against the ground nervously. Just as a cab began to slow down, a black tinted truck pulled up behind them. Hazel instantly knew who the truck belonged to because of the twenty-four-inch rims. It was Seven.

"Damn, there go Seven," Hazel grumbled as she tried to turn her head to hide that she was high. Seven parked behind the cab and jumped out. He had stubble on his face but it was lined up perfectly. He wore his hair so low that it looked bald, but he kept it perfectly lined also. His cowlick grew in the front of his head and it resembled swirls just above his hairline. Seven sported a Sean Jean leather coat that looked like it just came off of a Macy's rack.

"Let's go, Hazel," he said in his usual calm, low voice. He always spoke so low people usually had to concentrate on his lips to understand him. He walked around the car and onto the sidewalk where Millie was holding the cab door open.

"Hazel, get in the car," he demanded.

"I don't want to just leave Millie," she said in protest.

"Millie, I will take you where you need to go," Seven said as he looked at Millie.

"Cool," Millie said as she slammed the cab's door and thought about the cab fare she would be saving by hitching a ride with Seven. A seasoned dopefiend such as Millie cut financial corners as much as possible.

Hazel hesitantly got into the car, wishing that she never had run into Seven. Millie knew that he was going to throw a wrench in their plans to get high all day.

He acts like he is my man or something, Hazel thought as she sat in the car and crossed her arms, frustrated. Millie hopped in the backseat proudly as she lit up a cigarette and rolled down her window. Just as Seven was about to get into the truck, he saw Rico pull alongside of him on his motorcycle.

"Bitch, where my shit?" Rico asked as he clenched his teeth and had a murderous look on his face. Seven frowned up and followed Rico's eyes as he stared at Millie with hate. Rico had spotted them a block away and couldn't catch them before they got into Seven's car, which was their safe haven.

"What's the problem, li'l nigga?" Seven asked coldly as he looked back at Rico as if he was crazy.

"These bitches just robbed me!" Rico spat and he reached into his waist about to pull out his gun.

"You better calm yo' ass down," Seven ordered as he swiftly put his hand on Rico's, stopping him from pulling out his gun. "You already know," Seven confirmed, referring to Hazel's affiliation with him. Rico knew that Seven had loyalty to Hazel and he quickly calmed down, not wanting a problem with Seven. Seven is the one who supplied him with his dope and Rico didn't want any friction with the man who he looked up to. Plus, Rico didn't want any problems with him, being that Seven was the one who the whole block had shooters for days.

"I'm just saying, Seven. They robbed me for my dope about an hour ago!" Rico said, getting louder with each word. "I want my shit back now!" he said as he began to breathe hard. Seven looked into Rico's eyes, letting him know they were not on any friendly terms, and then looked at Hazel.

"Did y'all clip my man?" Seven asked as he looked into Hazel's eyes, knowing that she wouldn't lie to him. Hazel's heart was beating rapidly as she took her eyes off of Rico and looked into Seven's. She nodded her head to confirm what Rico had said.

"Fuck that li'l nigga," Millie shouted from the backseat, pointing at Rico wildly, and feeling real brave because Seven was around.

"Millie! Calm down," Seven said coldly as he shot a cold stare at her and instantly made Millie's mouth close.

"How much they take from you?" Seven asked as he looked back at Rico.

"About five hundred in dope and three hundred in cash," Rico lied, doubling each figure.

"And that's why you bitching?" Seven asked as he frowned up his face and blew Rico off by waving his hand at him. Seven grabbed his phone and dialed up his partner Raheem, also known as Rah-Rah.

"Rah, youngin' about to come through. Hit him with a quarter of something," he said just before he hung up the phone. Just like that, the problem was resolved. "Go to the spot and pick up that package. Stop getting caught slipping, li'l nigga. If you let yourself get 'got,' you deserved it," Seven preached as he got into the car and rolled down his window. "Don't even let bitch come out yo' mouth when you referring to Hazel, got that?" Seven asked rhetorically, not expecting an answer from Rico.

"Thanks, Seven," Rico said while he held his hand out, only to get ignored by Seven as he pulled off.

"What about me, Seven? He called me a bitch too," Millie asked teasingly while cracking up laughing in the backseat. "That li'l nigga was shook. Did you see his face?" she said as she clapped her hands together thinking about the frightened face Rico had made when standing in front of Seven.

"I didn't pay him back on your behalf. If Hazel wasn't involved, I woulda' fed yo' ass to the wolves. Believe that. I told you not to be having Hazel caught up in your little bullshit!" Seven barked in a low, stern tone as he maneuvered his truck down North Saginaw Street. He looked over at Hazel and knew that she was high by the way she was acting. She avoided eye contact with him and stared out of the passenger-side window as if she was in a trance.

Trying not to think about her putting needles into her arms, Seven brought up the reason why he was out looking for her that morning.

"I have been circling the block, looking for you all morning. Your father's visiting day is today. I'm on my way upstate to see him. I really want you to come with me. He's been asking about you," Seven said.

"Not today, Seven! Damn!" Hazel said as she grew tired of having the same argument with him.

"You need to go see that man. He loves you to death and you can't hold him down during his bid? You say that every time I ask you to ride up there with me. That's your father," Seven said, reminding her.

"Yeah . . . some father," she answered sarcastically as she thought about how he left her abruptly, just like everybody had done her entire life. Seven looked in his rearview at Millie who was in her own world. Seven couldn't see why someone who was as pretty as Millie could be a straight-up dopefiend. The drug had made her look older than what she really was, but you could still tell that she was a naturally beautiful woman. With her smooth, dark skin and full lips, she resembled the singer Lauryn Hill. Her kinky twists were on point and to the untrained eye, you would never be able to tell that she was a bad heroin addict. Her small, slim frame still made her a hot commodity for the dope boys around the way. Seven shook his head as he thought about the evil that women do. He wanted so badly for Hazel to break away from her, but no matter how much he told Hazel that Millie was bad business, she clung to her.

After a fifteen-minute drive, Seven pulled into the Carpenter Road Projects where Mille lived, a subsidized apartment complex that the government owned.

"Thanks, playboy," Millie said as she opened the door and stepped out. Hazel opened her door too, but Seven grabbed her arm and made her stay in the car. "You are going with me this time, Hazel. I'm not taking no for an answer," he said as he loosened his grip, not wanting to grab her too tightly.

"Okay, damn!" Hazel said as she folded her arms tightly. "I'll be back later," Hazel said as she looked at Millie. Hazel was mad, because she wanted to finish off the dope packs that they had stolen from Rico. She knew for sure that they would all be gone by the time she got back. *Fuck,* she thought as Millie closed the door.

"All right, Hazelnut. Love you!" Millie said as she walked toward the building with a peace sign held up. Seven pulled off, heading toward Jackson, Michigan to visit Hazel's father and his mentor, Apple.

Chapter Three

Hazel looked over at Seven as he drove on I-75. The smooth road and the effects of the drug had her drowsy. Hazel acted as if she hated to be around Seven, but actually she liked it. Seven was just twenty-four years old, but had the wisdom of an old head. Seven was a man of few words, but when he did speak, it was with power and conviction. Seven was all that a woman could want. He was young, very intelligent, attractive, and a certified hood nigga in every sense of the word. She knew Seven was out of her league and the only reason he cared so much about her, was the fact that she was Apple's daughter. Before Apple went to jail, he took Seven under his wing and treated him as a son. Hazel stopped staring before he noticed and looked out of her window.

"I hear you the man now. Look at li'l Seven. You all grown up now. Pushing heavy weight," Hazel said in a slurring voice with her eyes closed. The heroin still had a hold on her and was making her talk slowly and carefree. Seven glanced over at her and shook his head, not even wanting to respond to her.

"Look, get some sleep on the drive up there. You need to shake that shit off before Apple sees you. Look at you. You high as hell," he said, almost disgusted at her, while never even glancing back at her.

The mention of Apple's name made her think about when she first moved in with him as a young child. She closed her eyes and thought back when she was only seven years old. . . .

Hazel stared out the car window and watched as the unfamiliar houses briefly appeared into her view as she bypassed them. She was too young to understand the extent of what had just happened and unbeknownst to her, her life would never be the same. She had just seen Drena, her mother, lying in a casket, and witnessed her get put in the ground with dirt over her. At the age of seven, she couldn't understand why her mother was getting taken away from her. Apple, her father, tried his best to explain to her that she was "with God now," but that explanation still didn't enlighten Hazel's naïve mind.

"You all right over there?" Apple said as he glanced over at Hazel. Hazel briefly looked over at her father and nodded her head. She quickly went back to staring out of the window as Apple maneuvered his cocaine-white Lexus down Hill Road. Apple tried to figure out the best way to map out his next move. He had just been placed in a difficult situation. Although Hazel was his daughter, she was somewhat a stranger to him. Of course he took care of her financially, but he had barely seen her in all of her seven years on Earth. Hazel's mother was a dopefiend who Apple had slipped up and gotten pregnant while tricking with her as a teen. When Apple found out that she was pregnant he immediately denied Hazel. But once Hazel was born, there was no denying that she was his child. Apple had a mocha skin color and a big birthmark on his face. The mark was under his left eye and resembled an Apple, which is how he got his nickname. Hazel came out of her mother's womb with the same exact features. Her birthmark was a tad bit smaller than Apple's, but it was clear that she was his daughter. She was the female version of him. Apple would occasionally stop by and give Drena money for Hazel, but that was it. He never spent any quality time with her and didn't embrace what *responsibility came with fathering a child. Apple always was disappointed at himself for getting a dopefiend pregnant and tried his best to keep it short and sweet with her. Not wanting to be reminded of how careless and foolish he was for slipping with Drena, Apple had no relationship with his daughter. Nevertheless, now that Drena was gone, his hand was forced. He had to be a father to Hazel.*

Apple is what you called a hustler in every sense of the word. He ran packages up and down I-75, similar to FedEx, but the only difference was that Apple was moving raw heroin instead of packages. He wore the latest fashions and kept a thick, gold rope around his neck long before rappers made it famous to the world in the early '90s. Now that he had a daughter to take care of, he was lost. He didn't want to take her, but Drena had no family and he was the only option left. Apple did care for his daughter, but he knew that his current lifestyle wasn't fit for taking care of a minor. He was only twenty-five and in his prime. He had just met an out-of-town connect and was about to start making major paper, then this came.

Damn, what I am going to do with this girl? I don't know shit about kids, he thought as he *maneuvered the car on the road. He glanced* over at Hazel and just realized how innocent she was and how much she was going through. She had just lost her mother and he began to feel guilty for not wanting anything to do with her before.

"Hazel," he called. She looked over at him with her big brown eyes and long eyelashes while remaining silent.

"What do you like to do?" he asked as he gave her an uncomfortable smile. Hazel shrugged her shoulders and began to look out of the window once again. She was confused and the only thing she knew was that she missed her mother. Hazel was the one who found Drena in the bathroom with a belt wrapped tightly around her arm and a syringe sticking out of it. At first, Hazel just thought her mom was asleep, but after two days of no response she called the police. It seemed like Drena knew that her habit would catch up to her one day. Drena had always told Hazel if she ever couldn't wake her up to call 911. Hazel did exactly that, but this time Drena didn't come back . . . She was gone forever.

Apple pulled into the small house that he was currently residing in. It was a two-bedroom brick house that he had inherited from his grandmother. He rarely stayed there because *he was always on the move, but it was home to him. It was on the outskirts of Flint in a small, quiet town called Grand Blanc. He rarely let anyone know where it was because he never wanted karma to catch up with him and meet him at his front door. He made an exception for his longtime girlfriend, Tammy, who stayed there at times. He threw the car in park and took a deep breath as he rested both hands on the woodgrain steering wheel.*

"Okay, this is it. This is where you are going to be staying from now on," Apple said as he hit the unlock button, grabbed Hazel's small bag, and stepped out of the car. Hazel stepped out of the car also and stared up at the house in admiration. Although the house wasn't very big, in her eyes it was gigantic. It was a much bigger house than what she was used to with her mother. Hazel felt a hand on her shoulder; it was Apple.

"Come on, Hazel," he said as he walked alongside Hazel to the house. Once they got into the house, Hazel smelled the weed aroma as soon as she stepped in. She was familiar with the smell of weed at an early age. Drena had always had company over and they would smoke marijuana, along with many other drugs of their choice. Apple noticed the smell too and instantly knew that Tammy was in the back lighting up.

"Tammy!" he yelled as he closed the door and put Hazel's book bag by the door. "Sit down right here and I will be right back, okay?" he said as he grabbed the remote off of the coffee table and turned it to the Cartoon Network.

"Okay," Hazel said as she sat on the couch and stared at the TV.

"Oh, she does talk," Apple said sarcastically to Hazel as he smiled and handed her the remote control. Those were the first words Hazel had said to him all day. Apple faded to the back and left Hazel alone in the living room. Hazel looked around the foreign place and felt scared. She had never been away from her mother for more than two days, but since her death a week ago, Hazel was tossed into a situation that was traumatizing to a young mind. She had been staying with a neighbor until the day of the funeral where she was handed over to Apple. She didn't hate Apple, but she didn't like him either. She didn't even call him "Daddy." Drena called him Apple, so Hazel addressed him in the same manner, not knowing any better.

Hazel began to hear arguing from the back and with her nosey nature, she listened closely.

"What the fuck you mean? You brought the dopefiend's baby up in this bitch?" Tammy yelled with passion.

"You better calm down, ma. What am I suppose to do? She's my daughter!" Apple yelled back in protest. Tammy was uncomfortable with the fact that Hazel was there in the house. She always resented Apple for having a baby by Drena. Not to mention, Tammy was infertile and never could have a baby by Apple. She wanted to be the first one to birth his child, but his mishap with Drena messed that plan up. Tammy always resented Apple for that and she knew that if she had his baby, she would always have him. However, that was a feat that she couldn't perform.

"Take her to her relatives, shit! You know how much I went through with you when I found out Drena was pregnant and now you bring that little bitch up in here?" Tammy yelled.

"Watch yo' mouth, ma!" Apple said in a low but stern tone between his clenched teeth.

"Fuck that!" Tammy said as she put out her blunt in the ashtray and stood up. She put both of her hands on her wide hips and snapped her head back. "You are going to have to pick, Apple. It's me or her. I ain't the one!" she griped, getting more and more heated with every word. Jealousy had taken over Tammy's thoughts and all she saw was raging red. Apple couldn't believe that Tammy was giving him an ultimatum. Tammy had held him down since he was seventeen years old and although she got on his nerves at times, he did love her. Apple looked her up and down and admired her wide hips and slim waist. He loved the way her green eyes complemented her light skin and the way her hair resembled the short style of the singer Rihanna. He knew that she was dead serious and he was going to have to pick. Apple broke his silence and smirked.

"Tammy, you know I'ma pick my baby girl," he said, mentioning the nickname he would always call Tammy. He walked over to Tammy and gently placed his hand on the back of her neck.

"I'm glad you see things my way, baby," Tammy said as she smiled and looked into her man's eyes, knowing that she had charmed Apple into ditching his own daughter. She wanted Hazel out and out fast. She leaned in to kiss Apple, but he turned his head, making her lean into air. His grip got tight around Tammy's neck and he directed her straight to the door and into the living room toward the front door.

"My baby girl . . . Hazel. Get out, bitch, and respect the lady of the house," he said as he opened the front door.

"What the fuck you mean!" Tammy asked, not believing what she was hearing. Apple was throwing her out. "Hold up Apple!"

Apple glanced at Hazel who was looking at what was happening. Hazel had a small smirk on her face because she was glad that he was throwing Tammy out. Although she was young, she understood that Tammy didn't want her there.

"Tell this bitch bye, baby," Apple said as he looked at his daughter.

"Bye, bitch," Hazel said in an excited voice and with a big smile on her face as she gave Tammy a quick wave good-bye, obviously rubbing it in. Apple couldn't help but to chuckle at his witty daughter as he pushed Tammy out and slammed the door closed. He walked over to the couch, heavily breathing, and sat next to Hazel. He put his hand up and gave Hazel a high-five. Maybe this is going to work, he thought as they smiled at each other. They began to watch television together and laughing at Tammy who was kicking and screaming on the other side of the door. From that day forward, it was on. Apple and Hazel would eventually become inseparable.

Hazel snapped out of her dream and sat up, noticing that they were pulling up to the gated community known as Jackson Correctional Facility. She watched as a guard who sat in the booth leaned out of the window, asking Seven who he was there to see. Once Seven gave the guard the name of her father, he directed him where to park and opened the gates. Hazel's heart pounded rapidly as the nervousness built up in her chest. She hadn't been to see her father over the past years, not wanting him to see her in her current state. She was ashamed that she was a heroin addict. Heroin was the very reason her father was in jail, but not for using it . . . he sold it.

"I didn't tell him, if that's what you're thinking," Seven said as if he were reading her mind. "Get yourself together before we go in here," he instructed her as he looked at her wild hair and chapped lips. Seven reached into his backseat and pulled out a Macy's bag. "Here you go. I'm pretty sure this is your size,'" Seven said as he dropped the bag in her lap.

Seven stepped out of the car, giving her time to change clothes and respecting her privacy. A few minutes later, Hazel stepped out of the car wearing a two-piece jogging suit that fit her perfectly. It hugged all of her curves and she looked like a new woman. Unlike Millie, the drugs hadn't taken a toll on her body yet and she was still thick and shapely. She pulled her hair back tightly and her baby hair rested perfectly along her edges and she walked around the car, presenting herself to Seven.

"How I look?" she asked as she held her arms out, feeling good about herself as she barely could stand without swaying. Seven didn't even glance at her before answering.

"You look okay," he said unexcitedly as he started to walk toward the visitor's entrance. Hazel shook her head in disappointment and then looked at her backside and how she fit in her pants. She then followed him in. Her heart began to thump rapidly once again, thinking about seeing Apple for the first in a long time.

Thirty minutes later, they were through clearance and preparing to go into the booth to see Apple. Seven led the way as he looked for the booth D, where Apple was waiting. Seven smiled, something that he rarely did. Thick, five-inch glass separated them as Apple returned Seven's smile with one of his own. Before picking up the phone, Apple smiled and stared in Seven's eyes. He remembered when Seven was a youngster and idolized him. Apple always felt Seven was his son.

Seven's mother used to abuse drugs and even let her bisexual boyfriend have his way with him as she turned a blind eye to his pedophile ways. The stepfather sold heroin, so he had a hold on her that made her sacrifice her son's innocence at an early age. Apple was the one who supplied Seven's stepfather, Harold, with bricks of heroin. However, when Apple found out what was going on, he cut him off. Harold actually bragged about it one night while getting drunk with Apple. Apple quickly went into a rage and took Seven underneath his wing . . . after Harold mysteriously came up missing and, shortly after that, his mother died from a bad pack of heroin. Seven moved in with his grandmother and Apple kept up with him and always made sure he was okay.

He told Seven that he was about to start a new beginning and gave him the name "Seven" because that was the age that his new life started. His former name was Fredrick. At that moment that Apple told him that, Fredrick was dead and Seven was born.

Apple picked up the phone on the opposite side of the glass. "Hey, li'l man," Apple said, still seeing Seven as a little knucklehead who was always following him around.

"What up, Apple. How you holding up?" Seven asked.

"I'm doing as well as I can do," Apple answered.

"I miss you, big homie,"

"I miss you too. My friend who I introduced you to; is he treating you good?" Apple asked, getting straight to business, referring to the heroin connect that Apple set up for him.

"Yeah, very good," Seven said, giving Apple a small grin.

"Good, good. You remember what I taught you, right?' Apple asked.

"Always," Seven answered, referring to the advice he installed in Seven since he was a young boy. He would always say, "Play the game, don't let the game play you." Meaning to keep a low profile and get out of the drug game as soon he was financially able to. He didn't want Seven to end up in the same place he was currently at. "But look. I don't have a lot of time with you, so I want to show you something. It's a surprise," Seven said.

"What's that?" Apple asked in confusion as he rubbed his beard. Seven stood up and moved to the side as he hung up the phone. When he stepped to the side, Hazel stepped into view and sat down.

Apple dropped the phone from his ear in total shock and let it dangle. He paused in admiration. He stared at Hazel in complete awe. She was the most beautiful girl in the world in his eyes. Hazel had grown so much since the last time he had seen her. Apple was as hard as they came, but when it came to Hazel he was soft. She was his one and only soft spot.

Hazel took a deep breath and picked up the phone, sluggishly placing it to her ear. Apple stared at Hazel and gave her his charming grin, not believing how much she had grown. He hadn't seen her since she last visited him when she was a little girl. His heart was fluttering like never before.

"Hey, beautiful," he said as he looked deep into his only child's soul.

"Hey, Daddy," Hazel said as she noticed that Apple was getting older. The specks of gray in his beard displayed his age, but he was still as handsome as they came.

"I love you so much. You hear me?" he said as he emphasized every single word. His voice began to crack as he talked. Hazel nodded her head as she half smiled. She had forgotten how close they were before he left her abruptly. She tried to be more attentive, but the effects of using the drug caused her eyelids to seem heavy and made her sway in her seat involuntarily.

"I've been asking Seven to bring you up for a long time. He says he never could catch up with you," Apple said as he began to look closer at Hazel, who had begun to scratch her forearms.

She didn't even realize that she was doing it. The aftereffects of the drug had her skin crawling and her eyes were bouncing around. Apple knew that look oh too well. For a brief second, he thought that he was looking at Hazel's mom, Drena. Apple's heart dropped as he didn't want to believe that his baby had followed the footsteps of her drug-addicted mother.

"I just be so busy, you know. Going to school and all," Hazel lied, as she saw her father's sudden mood change and couldn't look him directly in the face because of her shame. Apple's voice began to crack again as he fought tears back and smiled trying to conceal his agony.

"Oh. What school are you going to?" he asked, playing along and knowing that she wasn't in school. Apple was dying deep inside. He couldn't believe that the rumors were true as he tried to keep a smile on his face, not wanting to spoil the visit by preaching to her. He had heard that his daughter had been using drugs but didn't want to believe it. But now the proof was in the pudding and it was killing him softly. Seven had yet to tell him that Hazel had turned to heroin, but he knew Seven was only trying to avoid putting the burden of knowing on him while he was serving a life sentence.

"Mott Community College," she lied. She dropped out of the school two years ago during the first semester because of her growing drug habit.

"I'm so proud of you, baby. You can be anything you want to be. Remember that," Apple said, having to grin to stop himself from crying. A tear slipped down his face involuntarily and he quickly wiped it away, trying to keep his composure in front of Hazel. His bottom lip began to quiver, but Hazel didn't notice it because she was so busy trying to avoid eye contact with him. Her eyes danced around and her drowsiness was evident. "Let me speak back to Seven before the time is up, okay, baby?" Apple asked as he put his hand on the glass. "I love you with all my heart and I always will. You are the best thing that ever happened to me, Hazel. You are the best part of me . . . my better half. You will always be my girl," Apple added as he witnessed Hazel begin to nod.

"Okay, Daddy. Love you," she whispered lazily, with her eyes closed, before she got up and handed Seven the phone.

Seven grabbed the phone and sat down, seeing the pain in Apple's eyes. That pained look quickly turned into a sinister stare as Apple leaned in closer to the glass as if he didn't want anybody to hear what he was about to say. Apple's eyes were watery and blood red.

"Seven. Listen to me and listen to me closely. That . . . woman . . . right . . . there, is all I have good left in this world. She is the best part of me and I refuse to let her do this. Listen! You get her off the streets, Seven! They're not fa' her. They're not fa' her," Apple said as he shook his head from side to side. Meaning every word, he stared at his protégé with sincerity and a burning passion, never blinking once.

Seven nodded his head in agreement, without saying a word. Seven had not seen Apple that hurt, nor had he ever seen him that angry. Seven knew that he owed Apple the world and he was determined to get Hazel right. Hazel had always refused his help, but now he was not about to take no for an answer.

"Make sure you bring her up here every month, when you come, all right? I love you, Seven," Apple said before hanging up the phone and putting his fist to the glass, as if he was giving him a pound. Seven returned the gesture and placed his fist on the opposite side of the glass, matching his. They both paused for a minute and Apple was the first to get up. The guard who stood behind Apple approached him and escorted him out. Seven watched as Apple got escorted out of the visiting area and until he couldn't see him anymore. Seven vowed to himself that Hazel would be his personal responsibility until she was clean. He owed Apple his life and wasn't going to let him down in any way.

"Let's go, Hazel," he said as he got up and grabbed her arm roughly, trying to snap her out of her nod as he led her out.

On the car ride home, Hazel fell into a deep nod once again and subconsciously she thought about her father. She thought back to a time when it was good for her finally and then. . . .

Jay-Z's classic album Reasonable Doubt *played as Apple and Hazel bobbed their heads to the music in unison, both mouthing the lyrics word for word along with the rapper. Hazel was twelve years old and she and Apple were closer than close. She was his Bonnie and he was her Clyde. Hazel thought about how Apple was teaching her things, but in actuality Hazel was teaching him life lessons. He learned responsibility and how to be a father from her. It had been five years since her mother passed and life was good for the both of them. Apple figured that since Hazel was with him permanently, he would teach her about life, no holds barred. He didn't lie to her about what he did, which was sell heroin, and they naturally became partners in crime.*

"Baby girl. How much is that?" Apple asked as he had on a doctor's mask, sitting at his kitchen table, cutting the dope with lactose and his special blend which remains to be confidential.

"We're at thirty-two thousand dollars, Apple," Hazel said as she put rubber bands around the G-stacks after she counted them. Apple had taught her how to count and put the money in "G-stacks," which meant a thousand dollars in each rubber band. Hazel could count faster and more accurately than any adult he knew. At age twelve she was a "professional cash counter," as Apple would say.

"We almost there, baby girl," Apple said as he glanced over at his daughter, who was in her pajamas counting money for him on that Saturday night.

"Almost there," Hazel repeated as she smiled and looked at her father. Apple had promised her that they would move to New York when he saved enough money to get out of the game. Hazel had a love for theatrical plays and the thought of being in New York was intriguing to her young mind. She always would see how

New York looked at night on television shows
and magazines. She admired the way the city
looked when lit up, and the "glamorous life" was
fascinating to her. Apple always told her "The
Big Apple" was named after him and would tell
her stories of how he used to go there to hustle
when he was younger, and shut the strip down
in an exotic car, with the thickest chain, and the
flyest clothes. His stories about the city were
legendary and instantly had her open.

"Apple, do they have mime shows in New
York?" Hazel asked as she remembered seeing
an old movie that had mimes on the New York
streets.

"Of course, baby girl. I'm going to take you to
the best mime show in New York! We are going
to stroll down the streets and you are going to
be rocking an expensive mink, baby girl! Them
mufuckas better watch out for Hazel Brown!" he
said as he temporarily stopped cutting the dope
and pulled down his doctor's mask, showing
Hazel his big smile. His comment made Hazel
light up and her heart fluttered thinking about
how fun it would be.

For the most part, hustlers would have another
woman count and rubber band his money for
him, but not Apple. Hazel was the leading lady
in his life and he didn't trust anybody but her.

Most people would consider Apple a bad father
for involving his daughter in illegal activities,
but in Apple's eyes he was spending quality time
with her. Hazel always loved to count Apple's
money, because she felt like she was a part of
something. While the normal American family
sat at dinner tables together every evening as
a source of bonding, Apple and Hazel counted
money and cut dope together on their Saturday
nights. Occasionally they would play dominoes
together. Apple would let her win every time,
loving to see her smack the last domino on the
table like a little gangster.

About an hour later, Hazel was just about
done counting Apple's monthly take. She filled
Apple's duffle bag up so that he could go and see
his connect to cop a few bricks of heroin. Hazel
put $50,000 in the bag neatly and zipped it up.
She took the rest of the money and put it in his
safe, which was on the floor in her bedroom
closet.

Apple was finally finished cutting his dope
with the lactose and went to the sink and washed
his hands thoroughly, hoping that this would be
his last flip. He looked at Hazel, who was returning to the living room and putting his bag and
gun by the door for him, so that he could hit the
highway soon. Apple never kept the clip in his

gun while at home, so he would have to retrieve it just before he left.

"I love you, Hazel," he said as he looked at the love of his life. Since the day he began taking care of her, he really began to understand the meaning of love; the love from a father to his child.

"Love you too, Apple," Hazel said as she looked at him and gave him her famous smile.

"Got a surprise for you," Apple said as he dried his hands off with the dishrag and walked toward her.

"Ooh, what is it?" Hazel asked excitedly as she clapped her hands together and jumped up and down cheerfully.

"Close your eyes," Apple said, smiling, going into the backroom and playfully tossing the rag at Hazel. Hazel lit up as she closed her eyes and waited to see what Apple had for her. Moments later she heard Apple re-entering the room.

"Hurry!" Hazel said as the anticipation built. She then felt something being laid on her shoulders and she quickly opened her eyes. She saw the mink coat and went crazy. "Thank you, Daddy!" she screamed as she rubbed the fur and spun around in it. Apple smiled, feeling so good that he was making her happy. It was the first time that she had called him "Daddy" and it brought joy to his heart hearing that word come out of her mouth. The mink was a tad bit too big for her, but she didn't care.

"You're welcome, baby girl," he said as he watched her prance around in the coat excitedly. "That's the same coat Princess Diana wore."

"Princess Diana? The princess?" she asked as she kept admiring the coat.

"That's right. But you're my princess," he said. Hazel couldn't stop smiling and she ran over and hugged Apple tightly as she laid her head on his chest. Apple held his daughter and realized that he had to get out of the game and make a better life for her at that point.

"One last flip," he whispered as he thought about getting out of the game for good. "Okay, Hazel, I am about to get ready to hit the highway. You are going over to Ms. Johnson's house for the night," Apple said, referring to his elderly next-door neighbor who occasionally watched Hazel when Apple took trips to re-up from his Arabic dope connect, Hassan.

"Okay," Hazel answered as she faded into the back room and gathered her overnight bag. "Thanks again, Apple," Hazel yelled as she admired herself in the dresser's mirror. She looked so glamorous. She could imagine herself in the city of New York, walking through the park with her father protecting her, while mimes did their acts for her. The scene in her head was just like a movie. She felt on top of the world in that all-white mink coat. Nevertheless, that good feeling would soon turn into anguish.

Later that night Apple was arrested while transporting two kilos of heroin on I-75. Hazel sat up and waited for her father, but he never returned. The next time she would see him would be at a prison, speaking through thick glass. That's when Hazel's world crumbled and the streets became her parents. The streets raised her and her life would never be the same.

Hazel snapped out of her dream, finally waking from her nod, and saw that they were almost near Flint. She smiled as she thought about how good she felt the night that Apple had given her the mink coat. It was the last good memory she had of him. That smile instantly died when she thought about what her life was like currently. She looked over at Seven and he seemed to be in deep thought, in his own little world. She looked at his strong jaw line and ebony brown skin and was starting to look at him in a different light. However, she flipped down the visor and looked in the mirror at herself. The bags under her brown eyes and her brittle hair confirmed that she wouldn't have a chance with him. The drugs had taken a toll on her appearance and she was looking more like thirty than twenty years old. *I got to get my shit together,* she thought as she sunk in her seat and waited to be dropped off.

Chapter Four

"What the fuck are you doing, you bitch-ass nigga?" Hazel asked as she kicked and screamed while Seven forcefully carried her up the stairs that led to his apartment. He picked her small frame up with ease and her bites, kicks, and insults didn't faze him as he thought about the task at hand. Once he pulled into his apartment complex and Hazel noticed that it wasn't Millie's place, she began to ask questions about why they were stopping there. He told Hazel that she was going to stay with him for a while and she instantly refused, so he took the matters into his own hands by forcing her.

Hazel wasn't thinking about anything but getting back to Millie's spot so she could get whatever was left of Rico's dope into her veins. Her body was itching for the good smack to tantalize it and Seven was hating on her high. "Get yo' damn hands off of me!" she yelled as an elderly black lady with curlers in her hair stepped out of her door to see what was going on.

"Everything's fine, Mrs. Dixon. Just go back in!" Seven ordered, still in his low, calm voice as he carried Hazel up while she threw constant blows at him. Still having Hazel clenched in his right arm, Seven reached the door, quickly put the key in the hole, and unlocked it. He pulled Hazel in and tossed her on the couch.

"Just calm down, Hazel," Seven demanded as he wiped the back of his neck to see if he was bleeding.

"What the fuck are you doing? Kidnapping me?" Hazel said as she quickly stood from the couch with her hands on her hips.

She breathed heavily as she tried to brush past Seven, only to have him grab her, stopping her in her tracks.

"Just calm down, damn," Seven said as he lightly pushed her back on the couch. "Look, we can do this shit all day if you want. But I'm not letting you leave. Not yet," Seven said as he held his arms out as if he was inviting her to try again.

"Fine!" Hazel yelled as she crossed her arms and flopped on the couch.

"You still bite your lip when you get mad," Seven stated as he grinned while noticing Hazel bite on her bottom lip.

Hazel didn't even notice that she was doing it until Seven pointed it out, and she immediately stopped. "Shut up!" she said as she picked up a pillow and threw it at him. She tried her best not to smile, but Seven knew that she had calmed down. She felt her high dying down and started to feel normal again.

"You hungry?" Seven asked as he walked into his kitchen that sat in the corner of his spacious threee-bedroom apartment.

Hazel didn't answer. She continued to fold her arms and thought about how Millie was getting high without her. There was no other place that Hazel would've rather been than on cloud nine, but Seven was determined on preventing that from happening.

What the fuck is this nigga problem? He doesn't own me. Why do this nigga care so much . . . damn! Hazel thought as she sulked on the couch. She watched as Seven locked the door from the inside with a key. *Damn, I can't get out without that damn key,* she thought as she grew even angrier. The heroin was calling for her and she wanted to get to it desperately.

Hours passed and Hazel had eased up a bit. She and Seven were sitting back talking about old times and how they used to hate each other as kids. Back then, Apple would go and pick up Seven and bring him to the house with him and Hazel at times. Hazel always had a little crush on Seven, but Seven was wise beyond his years. At the age of nine or ten he thought like an eighteen-year-old, so Hazel wasn't even on his radar. The only thing that was on his mind was becoming just like Apple.

Seven looked at Hazel, who sat on his couch Indian style while putting popcorn in her mouth. Music was playing in the background and they were both having a good time reminiscing while playing dominoes.

"You know, me and yo' pops used to play this all the time," Seven said as he cradled all his dominoes in his two palms and checked out what he had.

"Seriously? Me too. We used to play on Saturday nights and just chill and vibe out to music," Hazel said as a wave of déjà vu overcame her. She had just realized that she and Seven were doing the same thing she and Apple used to do. Hazel smiled and felt warm inside at the thought. That's when she realized that she hadn't had a good time like that in a long while. Hazel scooped up her dominoes like a pro, checking out her hand.

"What you got?' Seven asked, waiting for her to make her move.

"Don't worry about what I got, nigga," Bam! Hazel smacked the table, placing the domino on the board. "Gimme twenty," she said proudly and she gave him a big smile. Seven smiled, loving how hood Hazel was. He stared at her while she was writing her score down and he noticed how naturally beautiful she was. She was rough around the edges but if she got herself together she could be a very attractive girl. He quickly wiped away the notion when he thought about whose daughter she was. She was a far cry from his current girlfriend, GiGi, who was an upcoming big time model.

"You cool peoples," Seven said as he looked at the small apple-shaped birthmark on her face, which was a constant reminder of whose offspring she was.

"Yeah, you cool too," Hazel answered.

"I haven't chilled like this in a while. Nigga be so busy and all," Seven said as he placed a domino on the board.

"Ol' girl don't entertain you?" Hazel asked as she snapped her finger and looked into the air. "What's her name . . . CeCe?"

"GiGi. You know her name, ma. Stop fronting," Seven said as he slightly grinned and shook his head.

"Oh yeah, GiGi. That's her name. That high-yellow bitch be riding through the hood thinking she all that," Hazel said as she went her turn with the dominoes.

"Hater," Seven said, knowing it would get under her skin. They both laughed it off and chilled and talked about old times until Seven ended the night by giving Hazel his room while he slept on the couch. It was the first time Hazel had slept in a bed in a long time because she always fell asleep in dope houses or on Millie's small apartment's floor in the projects. That comfortable sleep would be short-lived because her boyfriend crept in and woke her up in the middle of the night.

Chapter Five

The crashing sounds of the thunderstorm echoed throughout the apartment and the thud of raindrops hitting the windowpane created its own soundtrack. Hazel's body shook and sweat dripped off of her back as her boyfriend, Heroin Jones, called for her. She tossed and turned in Seven's bed as she frantically scratched her arms, trying to stop the feeling of things crawling on her. Hazel still was asleep, but her Jones was wide awake. Her body called for the drug and Hazel began to scream loudly as the crawling feeling was getting too much to bear. Nightmares of bugs crawling all over her body had her terrified.

Moments later, Seven came in with only pajama pants on, displaying his built physique. He switched on the light and saw Hazel scratching herself vigorously, tossing, and turning frantically.

"Hazel," Seven whispered as he approached her. "Hazel," he called again as he sat on the bed and gently grabbed her, cradling her to stop her from scratching herself so hard.

"Nooo!" Hazel screamed while continuing to scratch herself so hard that she bled. She was still in her sleep.

"Hazel," Seven called in his low tone, but this time with more force. He began to gently rock her. Hazel never opened her eyes. She was having a bad nightmare, but she quickly began to calm down at the sound of Seven's voice and his warm embrace.

"Shh, You good, ma. You good," he said softly as he held her tight in his arms. Hazel eventually stopped tossing, and rested on his shoulders. Seven then gently laid her back down and watched as she began to lightly snore.

After watching her for a few minutes, he carefully stood up, trying to not wake her, and exited the room. He grabbed his pillow off the couch and returned to the room. He then lay on the floor, right next to the bed, and before long he was sound asleep too.

The smell of food cooking invaded Hazel's sleep and she sat up and stretched her arms above her head while yawning. She looked around, having to remember exactly where she was. She looked around the bed and saw traces of blood and instantly knew that she had been scratching herself while asleep again. She looked at her arms and saw the scratch marks to verify it. With her hair all over her head, she headed to the living room, following the smell. She entered the living room, which was next to the kitchen. She only had on panties and a bra, but she was far from shy and didn't mind. When she came out she saw Seven standing over the stove cooking, shirtless. He had a smooth, tattoo-free body and strong, broad shoulders. *Damn, Seven has grown up,* Hazel thought as she remembered back in the day when he had a bird's chest.

"Good morning," Seven said without even turning around. He had heard her creep in.

"Morning," Hazel said as she walked in.

"You want some eggs?" Seven said as he turned around with a pot in his hand. "Ooh!" he said as he quickly turned back around, turning his back toward Hazel. "You don't have any clothes on," he said, surprised.

"Boy, you act like you ain't never saw no titties before," Hazel said as she scratched her itching hair.

"Hazel, go put on some clothes. I have some shirts in my top drawer," he demanded as he never took a peek, keeping his back turned toward her. Hazel grew offended that he didn't want to look at her half-naked body. She had never met a man who turned down a glance of a naked woman.

"I guess," Hazel said just before she headed back to the room to get a shirt.

Seven shook his head from side to side as he began to fix their plates, leaving the sausage only for her plate. Seven was a vegetarian and didn't eat meat at all. It was a personal health decision rather than a religious one.

Hazel returned to the kitchen and sat at the table. Seven placed a plate in front of her and took a seat across from her so he could eat.

"Why are you doing this?" Hazel questioned, wondering why Seven was being so nice to her.

"Doing what?" Seven asked as he put a scoop of fruit into his mouth.

"Being nice and shit. Why are you trying to help me?" Hazel asked, trying to read Seven and find out his ulterior motives. "You must want something," Hazel said as she looked down at her breast, signaling that Seven wanted sex.

"Chill out, ma. It ain't that type of party, believe me. And plus, you're not my type anyway," Seven said as he kind of smirked after taking a look at her. Hazel instantly became embarrassed and felt that Seven acted as if he was above her.

"What the fuck does that mean?" Hazel retorted as she jerked her neck, getting louder.

"Nothing, ma. Look, your father was my hero. I told him that I would get you clean and that's what I intend on doing. Nothing more, nothing less. Eat your food, it's getting cold," he said as he watched her fold her arms, obviously angry at his comment.

"Whatever!" she said as she started to eat. "Anyway, thanks for helping me, Seven. I really want to get off that shit, ya know?" Seven's calmness made her calm and she decided to play nice.

"No thank you needed. We're just going to shake this shit off . . . together," he responded. Hazel smiled, feeling good about Seven having her back after she had avoided him for so long. Every time she had seen him in the hood, he would give her money and tell her that she needed to visit her father with him. Hazel would always blow him off, but he stayed persistent. He acted like he cared and it was finally getting to her.

"So, how did you get on that shit anyway? You grew up around that shit and knew what it does to a person, why would you do it?" Seven asked, trying to get a better understanding.

Hazel noticed how straightforward Seven was and he never beat around the bush. "It's a long story," Hazel answered as she took a sip of her orange juice.

"I have all the time in the world," Seven answered. Hazel closed her eyes and took Seven back to the night where she was formerly introduced to a boy named Heroin.

***

Hazel was sixteen and in a detention center for troubled teen females. Pasadena Girls' Detention Center was the name of the hellhole that Hazel called home for just over four years. After her father was incarcerated, Ms. Johnson gained custody of her but shortly afterward, she died from a heart attack. Things were never the same for Hazel after that. After numerous foster homes, Hazel couldn't get placed in a home because of her run-ins with the law. She got caught stealing from department stores on numerous occasions and the judge ordered her to a stint at the lock-up.

One of the counselors at Pasedena took a liking to Hazel. Her name was Millian Summers, a.k.a. Millie. Millie was straight out of the east coast and came to Flint in search of a better lifestyle. She was only twenty-six, not that much older than the girls she supervised. She landed a job at Pasadena and immediately became a role model for the female detainees. Millie was the youngest faculty member there, so she related to the girls more than any other counselor. Millie came in third shift to watch over them, the perfect schedule for a down-low and functional dope addict. She would take dope breaks in the wee hours of the night while everyone was asleep and it went unnoticed for over two years; that was, until Hazel stumbled upon her secret.

Hazel woke up in the middle of the night, suffering from a bad headache. The stress of being around hundreds of girls and their attitudes could do that to a person frequently. She left her dorm room in search of Millie, the only counselor on duty at the time. Hazel checked the front desk where the counselors usually stationed themselves, but Millie was nowhere to be found. Hazel looked around to see if anyone was looking, because she saw a perfect opportunity to take some Xanax pills. The pills were supposed to treat anxiety, but most of the girls there used it to get high. It made them feel lazy and on cloud nine if crushed up and taken through the nose. Hazel knew that she could get a lot of trade with the pills, so she jumped on the rare opening. She looked around to make sure the coast was clear and then reached over the desk and pulled open the desk drawer, where the staff kept the pills. She took out two bottles and stuffed them into her panties swiftly. "Where is Millie?" Hazel whispered as she looked around to see if she could get anything else from the desk while Millie was away. Hazel didn't see anything so she fled to the communal bathroom, not wanting to press her luck. She didn't want to return to the room, because her tattletale roommate would surely snitch her out if she saw the bottles.

Hazel was going to empty the pills into a piece of tissue paper and leave the pill bottles in the bathroom so she wouldn't have any evidence left in her room. Hazel zipped into the bathroom and quickly opened the door to the stall so that she could relieve herself of the bottles, but what she saw was like a flashback to her early childhood. She saw Millie sitting on the toilet with a needle sticking out of her arm. Millie was drooling from her bottom lip and slowly rocking back and forth as she looked like she was exhausted.

"Millie," Hazel called as she couldn't believe what she was seeing. It reminded her of the day she found her mother dead in the bathroom when she was just a little girl. "Millie," she called again, this time nudging her in the forehead lightly.

"Hey, Hazelnut," Millie slurred sluggishly after she glanced up at Hazel. "What you doing in here, baby?" she asked, high out of her mind. Hazel looked down at Millie and admired her pure beauty. She had no idea that she used drugs. Millie's appearance didn't seem as if she was a user, but all that glitters, sometimes, is not gold. She kept nice clothes and kept her hair done in the latest fashion. Her smooth dark skin was flawless, and to many of the girls in the detention center, she was their idol.

Hazel began to get an urge and she didn't know what it was exactly. The only thing she knew was that she wanted to try what was making Millie feel so good and what used to make her mother feel the same way. Hazel stepped back and walked to the bathroom door, locking it. She walked back to the stall and watched as Millie continued to rock back and forth in a dazed-like state.

"Can I try some?" she asked in the most innocent voice. She wanted to be just like Millie and share her joy.

"Sure," Millie said, not even realizing what she was saying or doing. Millie was feeling so good, so free that she didn't realize that she was giving her protégé death in the form of an addiction. Hazel slowly pulled the half-full syringe out of Millie's arm and took a seat on the floor next to her, leaning her back on the side of the stall. She instantly remembered how her mother would smack her arm trying to create a vein to shoot the dope in, so she emulated her, smacking her own forearm. Just like Mama, she thought as she smiled, thinking that she was becoming a woman. That was all she knew. The only two women who she ever looked up to got on the mystical dope train and she was about to jump aboard. Hazel wanted to experience that magic

ride also. In her mind, it was her rite of passage. By shooting the dope, she was becoming a woman in her young, adolescent mind. A big, green vein popped up after a couple of slaps and Hazel went to a place where only a dopefiend could fathom. A place so blissful, a place so cold, and a place so . . . dark.

Tears streamed down Hazel's face as she stopped telling the shameful story to Seven. She wished that night never had happened. It was the night that she got addicted to heroin and gave her life to the drug.

"Damn, ma," Seven said in disbelief as he stared into her teary eyes. He couldn't believe that she had been using since she was only sixteen years old. Seven usually would have looked down on a dopefiend, chalking it up to being weak-minded, but the way Hazel told the story it was as if it was her destiny. As if she had no control over the inevitable. He felt so sorry for her.

"So that's how it all started," Hazel admitted as she wiped her tears away and tried to shake the sadness off.

"That's deep. But you know what?" Seven said as he placed his hand under Hazel's chin and lifted her head.

"What?" Hazel answered as she looked at him in his brown eyes.

"That's the past. We going to get you off that shit, feel me? I got your back," he said sincerely as he grinned at her, trying to cheer her up. He remembered when she disappeared for a while and left the hood for the detention center, but he never knew that was where she picked up her habit. It all finally started to make sense to him. He didn't see her until years later when she got older and by then she was already so far gone.

"Thanks, Seven," she whispered as her voice cracked, displaying her pain. A man had never looked at her as more than a sex object and showed that he cared about her since the days of Apple. However, for some reason she felt safe with Seven. She truly believed him, but it was far more difficult to kick the habit than she could have ever imagined.

The clicking sound of Seven's deadbolt being unlocked echoed throughout the apartment. Hazel's and Seven's eyes shot to the door and seconds later, GiGi came strutting through the door with big, oversized shades on that added to her diva look. She wore a long peacoat and a Chanel rag on her head.

"Hey, baby. You got it smelling good in here," GiGi said as she began to pull off her coat without even looking at who was in the apartment. When GiGi finally did look up, she quickly snatched off her shades and snapped her head back. "Who the fuck is this bitch?" she asked with a heavy attitude.

"Betta get yo' bitch," Hazel whispered to Seven as she gave him a chance to save GiGi from getting the ass whooping of her life.

"What up, ma. Calm down. This is Hazel . . . Apple's daughter," Seven said, knowing that he had mentioned her to GiGi on numerous occasions.

"Hmph!" GiGi scoffed as she put her nose in the air and walked into the kitchen. "Nice to meet you," GiGi said sarcastically as she walked to Seven and kissed him.

"Likewise," Hazel answered as she continued to eat her food.

"Nice hair," GiGi added mockingly as she looked at Hazel's wild 'do.

"Betta get that bitch before she get fucked up," Hazel said under her breath to Seven while smiling. GiGi heard her and instantly caught an attitude.

"You got some nerve! I'm not going to even stoop to your level," GiGi said as she flipped her hair and stormed into the back room. "Seven!" she yelled as she disappeared into the back.

"Let me handle this," Seven said with a smile on his face. Hazel smiled back and continued to eat while shaking her head.

Seven went into the back and when he entered the room he saw GiGi with her arms crossed. Her left foot tapped the hardwood floor and she was heated.

"Why is that bitch in here?" GiGi whispered before she closed her lips tightly.

"It's not even like that, G. I'm just trying to help her out," Seven said as he approached her.

"What? You Captain Save a Ho now?" she asked.

"I ain't trying to hear all that. She is like a little sister to me. You know how much Apple means to me. I'm doing this for him. I gotta look out for her. She out there bad," Seven said as he stood over her, looking down into her eyes.

"Fuck that, Seven. She gots to go," she demanded.

"Or what?" Seven asked as he smiled and wrapped his arms around her waist. His deep, low baritone and fresh scent put GiGi in a trance-like state. "You ain't gon' leave. You love this dick too much," he said, knowing how to make her see things his way. Seven began to kiss on GiGi's neck and his hands fell down to her plump, round cheeks that resembled melons. He palmed them gently and massaged them in slow, circular motions, causing a moan to escape her lips involuntarily.

"You miss me? Tell the truth," Seven whispered in between kisses.

"You know I do," GiGi answered as she felt her spine tingle, and her love button began to pulsate at his touch. Seven always knew the right spot to touch and the right thing to say when GiGi was on her bullshit. Seven quickly scooped GiGi up by her behind and sat her on her oak dresser. She parted her legs, letting Seven into her personal space as they kissed passionately. Seven's hands found GiGi's neatly trimmed love box. She had a habit of wearing no panties and Seven loved that about her. Seven dropped his pants, already rock hard, ready for a stellar performance. He began to play with her love button with his thumb while slipping his two middle fingers in and out of her slowly. He then began to rub his tip on her button as he moved his hands away and let his soldier take over the job. He slowly slid into her, making her back arch in pleasure. She began to suck on his neck as she dug both of her nails into his back.

"Ooh, Seven, you so hard," GiGi complimented as he began to slow grind her, moving her ass better than a Latin dancer while inside of her.

Seven went deep, hard, and slow as he gradually made her forget why she was even upset. Seven knew by her silence that he was hitting her right spots. She didn't even worry about moaning or pretending that it was good, because she was too busy being in ecstasy. Seven was seasoned enough to know that if a man is hitting it right, all the moaning and dirty talk is nonexistent. That was all for show and Seven wasn't there to be playing. He was handling business. GiGi gripped his tight ass as he grinded her with a stroke of a genius, making her wetter with each pump. Slurping noises filled the room and Seven sped up, making her love box make noises.

"Right there, right there. Don't stop, nigga!" she crooned as she felt herself about to orgasm. Seven licked his middle finger and reached around so that he could play with her other hole, bringing her to a climax. He moved his finger in swift circular motions as her other entry got just as wet as her love box. GiGi smiled in pleasure as she enjoyed Seven's skills and perfect timing. She began to thrust her pelvis against him as she came closer and closer to her orgasm. "Seven!" she yelled as her love came down and a small squirt shot from her womb, dripping onto Seven's inner thigh. Seven instantly pulled out, not even wanting to get his orgasm. He just wanted to let GiGi know who the boss was. GiGi hopped off the dresser, staggered over to the bed, and collapsed.

"Seven, you the best," GiGi said as she breathed hard and waited for her legs to stop trembling. Seven smiled and smacked her on the ass just before he walked into the bathroom that was connected to his room.

"I have to hit the streets. Call me later, right?" Seven asked.

"Yeah, baby, I'ma call you," she said as she stood up and looked in the dresser mirror, fixing her hair.

"You still got an attitude?" he asked as he stepped in the shower. "Betta lose it and don't say nothing to that girl when you leave," he demanded.

"Okay, Daddy. I'm sorry. You know I get jealous sometimes," she said, standing up and straightening out her dress. "I am running late for a photo shoot in Detroit. I will call you when I get back," she said as she walked into the bathroom. She opened up the curtain and watched as he washed his body with the sudsy soap. "You hear me?" she asked.

"Okay. Talk to you later," Seven said as he closed his eyes, letting the water cascade down his face and onto his body.

"Okay," she said as she closed the curtain and left. She picked up her coat and saw Hazel washing her plate in the sink. Wanting to respect Seven, she said, "Bye." Hazel acted as if she didn't hear her and didn't even acknowledge her. GiGi shook her head and exited the apartment. Hazel caught an attitude as she thought about what she had just heard.

Why am I catching an attitude? Hazel thought while trying to convince herself that she wasn't feeling Seven. In due time, Hazel would stop faking and realize that Seven was the man of her dreams.

Thirty minutes later Seven emerged from the back, fully clothed. He had a tan sport jacket on with a tan casual dress shirt on underneath. The first button was undone on his shirt but he still looked neat and debonair. The casual yet sophisticated hook up he had on made him look like he had just jumped out of a *GQ* magazine. His neatly ironed slacks and crisp loafers only added a cherry on top of his debonair look. Seven carried a duffle bag in his right hand, ready to go handle business. Hazel was watching television as he entered.

"Okay, Hazel, I'm about to head out for a couple of hours.

Make yourself at home and there is food in the fridge. We will talk later this evening and I will take you shopping then, cool?" he asked as he headed to the door.

"Why are you being so good to me, Seven? You know you don't have to do this," Hazel said, not understanding his loyalty to her. Hazel turned around and took a look at Seven and couldn't believe that Seven was looking so professional, totally the opposite of his hardcore persona. Seven pulled out a pair of non-prescription, sophisticated-style glasses and slid them on, making him look more like a doctor than a drug dealer. *Damn,* Hazel thought, amazed at his new appearance. Seven gave her a small grin and opened his door. Seven was on his way to meet his connect and transport a few bricks of heroin from Canada back to Flint. He only wore professional attire to stay off the police's radar while moving the weight up and down the highway, a mistake that Apple made that wouldn't go in vain.

"See you later," he said as he left, not answering her question. Seven disappeared into the hallway and closed the door, leaving Hazel there alone. Hazel felt like a little child again as she watched Seven walk out the door with a bag full of money, just like Apple used to do.

Chapter Six

Seven cruised the highway with Rah-Rah on his passenger side. It was the first of the month and it was time for Seven to go cop from his out-of-town connect. Rah-Rah sat, sunk low in the passenger side with a black .45 pistol on his lap while he moved the toothpick around in his mouth with his tongue. Rah was black as night with smooth skin and a full beard that came three inches off his face. A three-sixty wave pattern graced his head and added to his neat look. Rah-Rah was Seven's shooter, his enforcer, and right-hand man.

"So you fucking her or what?" Rah asked bluntly as he wondered about Hazel, who was back at Seven's apartment. Seven, always the one to choose silence over an explanation, remained quiet and smiled as Rah tried to get the 411. "Man, I know you hitting that," Rah said, trying to convince himself. Seven just shook his head and smiled at how curious Rah was. "All the years I have known you . . . You never let a chick move in with you. Not even GiGi," Rah said, referring to his current girlfriend.

"How those niggas over in the fifth ward moving through them joints?" Seven asked, quickly changing the topic of conversation. He was referring to the bricks of heroin that he had fronted them a couple of weeks back.

"They are done with the first shipment. The young boys over there getting it. They just called me to re-up again." Rah said, nodding his head in approval. Seven was the man who brought all the dope into Flint, but he let Rah be the front man. Seven just sat back and collected the money like a true boss should; just as Apple had taught him.

"Cool. And the south side boys?" Seven asked.

"They paid yesterday. They ready for some more joints too," Rah answered. Seven could already feel the money in his hands, which made the trip they were taking to Canada all the more sweet. They just passed Detroit preparing to get on the Canadian bridge that separated Canada and Detroit. Rah-Rah also dressed in professional wear trying to hide their gutter appearance from any suspecting police just in case they got pulled over. The dummy gas tank under Seven's coupe was empty, but not for long. Soon it would be jam-packed with Saran-wrapped heroin bricks, making the car a few kilos heavier.

Meanwhile in Seven's apartment, Hazel walked back and forth, pacing the floor anxiously, while clenching her stomach, contemplating larceny. She was itching for her first shot of the day. Her stomach was in knots and bubbling as she grimaced, waiting for the pain to settle. She had been to the bathroom about five times since Seven had left. He had only been gone two hours, but even that was too long. Her bowels were getting the best of her and she couldn't stop herself from feeling like she was about to go on herself every five minutes. "Fuck!" she yelled as she grabbed her own hair while still pacing.

"I can't do this shit," she said, trying to talk herself out of what she was about to do. Seven's forty-two-inch plasma television was calling her name. She knew that she could get a pretty penny for it, and internally her conscience was having a battle. "I can't take this shit. He's trying to help me though," Hazel said, battling with her conscience as she tried her best to not look at the TV.

"I can get about five hundred for that for sure," she said to herself as she began to scratch her arms as they felt like ants were crawling all over them. A sharp pain shot through her stomach once again, this time knocking her to her knees. Hazel began to cry as she balled into a fetal position in excruciating pain.

Once the throbbing subsided, Hazel jumped up and went for the television. As she unplugged all of the cords, the only thing she could think about was shooting the dope into her veins and stopping the pain she was feeling. Using heroin was a full-time job. If a person doesn't have it in their system, their body will let them know and Hazel was feeling it full strength.

"Sorry, Seven. I'm so sorry," she whispered as she unplugged the television, yanking the cords out of the socket. Seconds later, she struggled with the television and headed out the door on her way to the hood to sell Seven's property. Fuck a monkey; she had to get that gorilla off of her back. She was about to catch a cab over to Millie's apartment to put her up on the stolen goods.

"Stop playing, nigga. Damn! This mufucka go for about two thousand dollars at Sears," Millie said as she tried to sell Seven's television to a hustler who sat in the dope house. Hazel stood behind the TV, letting Millie broker the deal.

"Well, this ain't no fuckin' Sears, as you can see. You gon' take it or leave it? I'll give you two packs for that mufucka," the hustler said as he eyed the television. Millie and Hazel had been trying to get the TV off for over an hour and both of them were already jonesin' badly.

"Man, fuck it. Take that shit, Millie," Hazel said as she gripped her stomach and shifted her weight from one foot to the other one. Hazel didn't care that she was trading a two-thousand-dollar TV for a hundred dollars worth of dope. She just wanted to get her fix so she could stop the excruciating pain in her stomach. She knew that she was seconds away from using the bathroom on herself but she wanted to see the deal through before rushing to the stool.

"You's a old bitch-ass nigga! You know this shit worth way more than what you offering," Millie said as she snatched the two packs of dope off the table, which he had set there to entice them. As soon as Millie got the dope in her hand, they both dipped into the back room, which was one of the only remaining free rooms left in the crowded dope house. Using the bathroom was the last thing on Hazel's mind as she anticipated shooting up.

"Come on!" Hazel demanded as she began to pull down her pants so that she could find a vein

in the crease next to her vagina. She didn't want
to use her arm, because she had used it the day
before and she liked to switch it up so that she
wouldn't overuse the same spots. Millie sat at the
table and began to set up. She emptied the dope in
a spoon and pulled out her syringe that was in her
purse. She sucked the water from a bowl that was
at the center of the table. Hazel's eyes lit up as she
thought about where she was about to go. Millie
looked into Hazel's eyes and saw no depth. Millie wanted so badly to tell Hazel to leave the drug
alone, but she knew how it felt to have a monkey
on your back. Millie wanted to cry every time she
did drugs with Hazel, but the sad feeling always
was trumped by the thought of the ecstasy that
the drug provided. Millie helped Hazel tighten the
belt around her thigh and they both took the cold
train to cloud nine.

   Seven and Rah pulled up to the humungous
house that sat on the lakefront in a small suburb
just miles away from the Canadian bridge. The
house sat back a couple of acres from the curb
and was a spectacular sight to see. It was something that Seven was looking forward to having
one day. As they pulled up the long driveway,
two beautiful Asian women with long, flowing

hair came out the front door, both wearing black dresses and six-inch heels.

"Damn, are they twins?" Rah asked as he stared at their tight, petite bodies and small, firm asses. When Seven stopped the car, one lady went on each side and opened the door for them.

"Hello, gentlemen. Welcome," the lady on Seven's side said with a perfect smile and a flawless English accent.

"What up, ma," Seven greeted as he stepped out, handing her the keys so she could park his car in the back. Seven loved the way Hassan was living. It was a residence, but Hassan had a valet-type system with gorgeous women as valets.

"Right this way, gentlemen," the other Asian woman said as her twin sister got into the driver's seat and pulled the car around. "Hassan has been waiting on your arrival," she said as she began to lead them to the twelve-foot front door. Rah fell behind, trying to get a good view of the woman's assets while being escorted into the house. When they entered the house, the sound of Prince's song "Soft and Wet" lightly played throughout the mansion's speaker system and the mixed smell of weed and incense danced through the air. The well-lit, spacious front room was equipped with marble floors that were so shiny they looked as if they had a layer of glass on them. The high ca-

thedral ceilings were thirty feet high and painted
with Arabian angels, all of them resembling Hassan's face. The mansion never ceased to amaze
Seven and Rah as they looked around and saw
many women of different nationalities walking
through the mansion; all half naked. The skimpy
silk robes and exotic negligees were enticing to
any man who walked in. It was as if Hassan was
the Arab version of the infamous Hugh Hefner.
His home was crawling with beautiful women and
he was living every man's fantasy. Moments later,
Hassan came down the stairs with his all-white
terry cloth robe on, complimented by Ferragamo
suede house slippers on his feet. A glimpse of his
abundance of chest hair peeked out the opening
of his robe. Hassan had olive-colored skin and
his long hair was neatly combed back into a
ponytail that fell to the middle of his back. His
Arab heritage was very evident in his physical
features. Hassan had perfectly manicured nails
and feet because of his metrosexual tendencies
and narcissistic views on life. He approached
Seven and Rah while smiling and extending his
hand to Seven.

"Good evening, my friend."

"Hello, Hassan," Seven answered as he shook
Hassan's hand firmly. Hassan nodded his head
at Rah, but didn't speak to him. He focused his

attention back on Seven and opened his hand, waving it toward the den that sat in his tri-level mansion.

"Shall we?" Hassan asked as he led Seven toward the den. Seven leaned over to Rah and told him that he would be right back after negotiating with Hassan. Rah rubbed his hands together and stared at the thick Latino woman coming down the stairs in lingerie, and had no problem being left unattended. His eyes were glued on her huge breasts and her long-pointed nipples that showed through her see-through garments. Rah always loved to come to Hassan's place with Seven. Hassan's palace was like a 24-7 orgy waiting to happen and with Rah being a freak and all; he was in paradise.

"Take your time, fam. Take your time," Rah said as he began to follow the ass and perky, plastic-surgery tits into the main room.

Seven followed Hassan into the den, which was on the lower level of the house. As Seven went down the stairs that led to the den, he noticed the mood and decorative theme had changed. The speaker system was turned off in the lower den and the all-white carpet made it look immaculate. The carpet was so soft, Seven felt like he was walking on pillows as he went across the floor. The Italian, white leather couches equipped with round, glass in-tables, and a huge plasma television that hung on the wall were nothing short of amazing.

"Have a seat, my friend," Hassan offered as he took a seat on the couch, right across from Seven.

"I need two whole things and was wondering could you spot me two on consignment," Seven said, getting straight to business.

"I see that you are trying to step your game up, Seven."

"Something like that. I am ready to make some power moves. I just need to start thinking about the future."

"You're a smart man. You remind me so much of Apple. I just wish that he had been thinking the same way you were thinking back then," Hassan replied. Apple was on his way back from copping from him when he got busted years ago.

"Yeah, me too."

"I tell you what. You say you want two kilos on consignment. I'ma give you ten. It's time to step you up into the big leagues. You have been buying from me for years and every time you come, you just buy a few at a time. Usually I would have cut you off as a customer, but Apple spoke very highly of you and off the strength of him . . . I fucks with you. But it's time for you to do this right," Hassan said as he glanced at the tall, slender Russian woman who came into the room heading straight for the bar. Her hair was short and white as snow. She began pouring Hassan his favorite drink: Scotch on the rocks.

Seven nodded his head in agreement as he began to rub his hands together thinking about the opportunity that Hassan had just placed in front of him. The woman brought the drink to Hassan and asked Seven if he wanted something. Seven shook his head no and focused back on Hassan.

"I'm ready, fam," Seven said, looking forward to shutting the whole city of Flint down with the raw he was about to get hit with.

"Great," Hassan said as he took a sip of the drink and looked at the Russian woman. "Get ten kilos for our friend." Seven smiled and put his plan to flood the city in motion.

Rah looked down at his rod getting slurped by the Latino he took a liking to earlier and rubbed the breast of another woman who was sucking on his nipples. Every woman in Hassan's mansion was an avid ecstasy pill popper, so it didn't take long for Rah to get his freak session popping off. Seven and Hassan returned to the main room, Seven having a duffle bag in hand. Seven shook his head as he saw Rah grinding his pelvis into the beautiful woman's mouth. Rah's eyes were closed and Seven chuckled at how Rah was so into it, with small sweat beads on his nose.

"Rah, let's roll," Seven said in his low voice. Rah didn't even hear him. "Rah!" Seven said louder, getting his attention.

"Hold on, fam," Rah begged, not taking his eyes off the girl who was pleasing him. Hassan, being a nymphomaniac himself, walked behind the woman who was sucking Rah and opened his robe, exposing his hairy, naked body underneath. Hassan licked his two fingers and began to rub on her holes, searching for her womb. The girl, without hesitation, parted her legs and propped her ass up in the air for easier access. The ladies in the room flocked to Hassan as if he were a magnet, caressing him and each other all at once.

"Damn, man," Seven said as he turned his head, not feeling comfortable with the orgy forming right before his eyes. "Fuck it, I'ma load up," Seven said as he headed to the parking garage so he could load the dope in the dummy gas tank. His mind was always on the money, never on pussy. That was why he was the boss and Rah was the help. "Let's get it," Seven whispered to himself as he faded into the darkness that led to the garage.

Chapter Seven

Seven pulled into his apartment complex and was dead tired. It was 1:00 A.M., and he had just dropped off Rah, leaving him with every brick except one, which was promised to one of his south side buyers, Mouse. He was supposed to meet up with Mouse first thing in the morning, so he kept the brick on him. He threw his car in park and exited the car, having the brick tucked in his inner coat. He hoped that Hazel was still up so they could kick it for a minute. He felt bad for leaving her there alone all day. *I know she was bored*, he thought as he climbed the steps that led to his apartment's door. He unlocked the door and stepped into the dark apartment. When he flicked on the lights, his heart dropped. He saw that his television was gone. The cords were sprawled over the floor, where Hazel had ripped them from the back of the television. He already knew what had happened. "Damn, Hazel," he whispered as disappointment overcame him. He shook his head from side to side and walked over to the kitchen. He grabbed the empty Cheerios box and then stuffed the brick of heroin into it. Although he was tired and upset, he went to look for Hazel. *What did I get myself into?* he thought as he headed out the door, knowing exactly where Hazel was.

Hazel smiled while her eyes were almost closed. She was high as a kite in the middle of the dope house as she lay slumped on a dingy beanbag chair. Fiends were scattered all over the spacious house doing their preferred drug, while the dope boys sat at the middle table waiting to serve anybody who wanted more. She looked in the corner of the room and saw Millie's slim, naked body grinding on the lap of a young hustler, giving him the ride of his life. Her small breasts bounced up and down as she demanded the attention of every dope boy in the house with her loud moaning and on-point rhythm. The sound of her ass landing, smacking against his balls filled the air. "Damn, Millie," another hustler yelled as his eyes were fixated on her petite, plump behind moving in fast circular motions. Her wetness was dripping off of her love box and she grabbed her small breasts and stretched them by gripping them, so she could suck them herself. Millie knew exactly what she was doing, which was making a commercial for herself; to the other hustlers. With them lusting after her and seeing her skillfulness, she would never be dope-less, because her sex would be a hot commodity throughout the hood. Hazel couldn't wait until the young hustler reached his orgasm, so that they could start using the pack that he promised to Millie as a trade for the sexual favor. The sound of the young hustler grunting sounded throughout the room as he stretched his legs straight out. Millie hopped off of him quickly, exposing that he didn't have a condom on. His load shot out of his rocket and onto his own hands and inner thigh. Millie immediately held her hand out, waiting for her payment while juices dripped from her love box. The hustler shook his rod off and quickly put it back in his pants, not wanting to have his pole on display for everyone. He then dug into his pockets and gave Millie a fifty pack while he sweated and breathed heavily, giving the dope up gladly.

Millie turned around and looked for her pants, exposing her chubby vagina, which hung low and was so fat that it didn't match her petite frame. Her lips were swollen and glazed as every man in the room took a peek at her chunky monkey. She grabbed her pants and slid them on quickly and waved over Hazel, so they could slip in the back room and shoot up. Millie faded into the back, anxious to see what the dope was like. Hazel slowly got up and began to follow Millie into the back room, but a hand stopped her from going. It was the hustler that was cheering Millie on earlier. He was hard as a missile and it showed through his baggy sweat pants. He wanted a piece of Hazel after seeing what her girl could do.

"Hold on, ma. Let me hit that," he demanded as he dangled a bag of dope in his free hand. Hazel quickly snatched her arm away from him and smacked her lips. She never had traded sex to feed her habit. That was Millie's thing, not hers.

"I'm good, playboy," Hazel said as she tried to walk away. But the young hustler snatched her back, making her fall into his lap. He instantly began to grope her and feel her nice-sized breasts. "Stop," she protested lazily as she tried to defend her body from his touches. The other hustlers were laughing at her trying to block his gropes, but all the laughing stopped when Seven came through the door with his own key, being that it was his own dope house that he had set up for his runners.

The young hustler who was groping Hazel didn't notice that everyone had stopped laughing because he was too busy ripping Hazel's shirt off. It wasn't until he felt the cold steel of Seven's gun striking him that he knew what time it was.

"Aghhh," the young hustler yelled as he held his bloody ear. He quickly went for his gun and stood up to see who had clocked him, but he immediately lowered his weapon when he looked into the eyes of a killer. "Damn, Seven. I didn't know that was you," he pleaded as he continued to hold his aching ear. Seven looked at Hazel, who was on the floor trying to cover herself up.

"Hazel, it's time to go!" With dominance, Seven grabbed Hazel's arm and helped her off the floor. Seven had set up that specific house for his young hustlers to post at while they served his dope; never did he imagine that he would provide Hazel a spot to poison her body. "Everybody listen up," Seven said in a rare loud tone, so everyone could hear him. "You see this girl right here?" he asked as he jerked Hazel by the arm, and then paused, making sure every pair of eyes were on him and Hazel. "Nobody serves her! Nobody!"

Millie came out of the back room with a belt tied tightly around her arm with her pants unbuttoned showing the hair beneath her belly button. She wanted to see what was taking Hazel so long, but she quickly realized what had happened when she saw Seven's face. "Damn," she whispered, knowing that he was there to rain on their parade.

"I knew it," Seven whispered when he saw Millie step out. "You stay away from Hazel or I'ma kill you. Try me if you want to," Seven said, meaning every word of it. Usually you couldn't pay Millie not to talk shit, but she saw the look in Seven's eyes and opted to remain silent, not wanting any parts of him at that moment. "Like I said, nobody serves Hazel or I'ma cut you off. If I hear about any of you niggas serving Hazel . . . no dope for nobody. Then nobody can make any money. I will come and sell out this mufucka if I have to and cut all y'all out the picture. Understand!" Seven said as he took his time and eyed each of the five hustlers who were present. Seven controlled that whole hood and without his dope, it would be a drought. The young hustlers knew who the boss was and from that point on, it would be also impossible for Hazel to cop from her old neighborhood. Her only other option would be to go to the south side to cop, which was a twenty-minute drive or a two-hour walk. Seven dragged Hazel out of the dope house and back to his place. It was the beginning of a long journey, but he was determined to get Hazel back right.

The next morning Hazel woke up to the sound of drilling and with a slight headache. The previous night was like a blur to her. The only thing she remembered was that one minute she was high, feeling good at the spot, and the next minute, Seven was pulling her clothes off and laying her down to sleep in his bed. Of course, Seven slept in the living room again. While rubbing her temples, trying to ease her headache, Hazel groggily entered into the living room and saw that Seven was sweating, shirtless, while drilling a four-by-four over his windows that led to his fire escape, which made it impossible for Hazel to slide a television out again. He was taking every precaution, not trying to make the same mistake twice. Hazel also noticed that Seven's television was back in its original spot. He greeted her without turning around.

"Morning," he said in his usual low tone.

How does he do that? "Good morning. You mad at me?" Hazel asked, feeling ashamed of what she had done the previous day.

"No. Not mad at all. I already knew that was going to happen. I have been dealing with dopefiends all my life. I guess I just was hoping that I could change you in a day," Seven said as he finished putting the first board up and wiping the sweat from his brow. Hazel felt horrible about what she had done and decided to give Seven an explanation.

"Seven, can I ask you something?" Hazel said as she sat on the couch, watching him walk right past her. Seven didn't have anything to say to Hazel and was making it obvious that he was trying to avoid eye contact with her. He knew that if he thought about her stealing from him, he would get upset at her disloyalty.

"Yeah, go 'head," Seven said as he grabbed more nails that were on the kitchen table. When Seven walked past Hazel to return to drilling, she grabbed his hand.

"Seven! Just stop for a minute. Do you know how it feels to crave heroin, huh?" Hazel asked as she gripped his hand tightly and began to tear up. The saddened look on her face made Seven lighten up, and he sat down on the couch next to her.

"No, I can't say that I do." "Well, it takes over your body. If it's not in your system . . . it feels like you're dying. Sometimes I can't even control my bowel movements, Seven." Hazel was giving him the ugly truth, not holding anything back while demonstrating complete humility. Hazel buried her face in her hands as the tears began to roll down her cheek. "I can't help it. When I start getting that Jones, I don't think straight. The only thing on my mind is getting that shit in my veins. I don't care who I have to hurt, steal from, or betray to get it. I'm so sorry. I . . ." Before she could even say the rest of her sentence she began to hyperventilate and cry like a newborn baby. She was breaking down right before Seven. He couldn't help but to feel sorry for her. He replaced his hand on her back and then began to rub.

"Damn," he whispered to himself.

"This shit got a hold of me. I want to shake it so bad."

"I am going to help you get through this. But you have to help me help you. I can't hold you down if you steal and lie," he whispered, but spoke just loud enough for her to hear him. Seven knew that he would have to be more hands-on in helping her with her recovery. He went and got the phonebook, searching for professional help for Hazel. He knew he couldn't do it alone.

GiGi was acting overly nice to Hazel as she sat in the living room with her watching a movie. Seven had asked her to come over and take Hazel shopping while he made a run up the highway. Seven left GiGi with $3,000 for Hazel, but Hazel only saw 500 of the dollars. The rest went in GiGi's pocket. Nevertheless, Hazel was appreciative and she got some nice clothes with the money. Hazel couldn't understand why GiGi was acting so nice to her and chalked it up to a change of heart. Hazel was wary at first, but then after a couple of hours she got comfortable with GiGi. GiGi began to quiz Hazel about her and Seven's relationship. Hazel told her truth, stating that it was like a brother and sister relationship: nothing more, nothing less. After hours of sneak interrogating throughout the day, GiGi couldn't come up with any anything incriminating in stone, so she grew angrier by the second. GiGi had a jealous streak a mile long and was determined to get Hazel out of Seven's life. *I hate this li'l bitch. I don't know what Seven sees in her dopefiend ass,* GiGi thought as she got up and headed to the refrigerator with a fake smile plastered on her face. GiGi stood behind her and stared. Jealous thoughts emerged and she thought about how she could get rid of Hazel. GiGi knew how Seven felt about Apple. Seven was big on loyalty, so GiGi thought about ways to make Seven feel as if Hazel was untrustworthy to get Hazel out of the picture. All of a sudden GiGi got an idea. It was as if a light bulb popped on in her head and she smiled and put the tip of one of her manicured nails in between her teeth sinisterly.

"I'm hungry as hell," GiGi said loudly. "How about you?" GiGi asked, waiting for Hazel to fall into her trap.

"Nah, I'm good," Hazel answered as she was deep into the good movie playing. GiGi walked over to the refrigerator and moved around a couple of boxes that sat on top of it until she found the one she was looking for.

"What's this?" GiGi asked loudly as she pulled down the box that she knew Seven kept extra bricks in. She had seen him put it in there before when she was pretending as if she was asleep. She knew that it would be impossible for a dopefiend like Hazel to turn down dope if it's available.

"What's what?" Hazel said as she looked back.

"This," GiGi said as she pulled out a plastic-wrapped brick of heroin with a "*Lady Luck*" stamp on it. Hazel's eyes quickly grew big as she saw what was in GiGi's hand. Hazel quickly got up and walked over to her cautiously as if GiGi held a bomb in her hands. Hazel's eyes were fixed on the brick, and GiGi smiled seeing the thirst in Hazel's eyes. GiGi had Hazel right where she wanted her.

"What's this shit?" GiGi asked again, playing dumb.

"GiGi, I don't think you should mess with that. Put it back where you found it," Hazel said as she tried to prevent herself from looking so fascinated. Hazel knew how good *Lady Luck* was and her forearm instantly began to itch as she thought about how it would feel if it was surfing through her veins. Hazel closed her eyes and looked as if she was having an orgasm, and GiGi was watching, nodding her head in enjoyment.

"What is it?" GiGi asked again.

"Nothing! Just put it back before Seven gets home," Hazel said as she snatched it out of her hands and put it back in the cereal box. Hazel then placed the box back on top of the refrigerator. *This green bitch! She don't even know what dope look like,* Hazel thought as she shook her head and returned to the couch along with GiGi. They continued to watch the movie, but after seeing the package, Hazel couldn't focus on anything else but getting high. GiGi smiled on the inside knowing that Hazel would eventually self-destruct. She had set the bait; now all she would have to do is wait for Hazel to take it. GiGi knew that Seven would surely kick her to the curb at the moment he found out that she would steal from him.

Chapter Eight

Seven, with Hazel, pulled into Insight, a rehabilitation center for women. Hazel had begun to scratch herself and the excruciating stomach pains had already begun. She hadn't used in the last couple of days and it was getting to her. Seven had been right by her side as she got cold sweats, shook, and trembled as she went through withdrawal. The only time he left her side was to briefly pick up his money from his dope spots, but he would always come right back, not leaving her alone for more than an hour at a time. Seven called around the city and managed to get her into a program that aimed to get dope addicts off of heroin, and today was her first scheduled day to attend the outpatient program.

"You are going to be all right," Seven assured as he put his truck in park and looked over at Hazel. Hazel took a deep breath and gave Seven a forced smiled as she felt her stomach doing somersaults from her nervousness, among other things.

"I'll go in with you," Seven offered.

"Thanks," Hazel responded as they both got out of the car and headed into the facility together. Hazel stayed close to Seven as they walked in, as if she were a little girl trying to hide underneath her father. Seven approached the middle-aged white woman who was at the front desk; obviously the receptionist.

"Hello, may I help you?" she asked.

Seven smiled and answered, "I called last week. I am here to admit Hazel Brown for treatment," he said in his low tone.

"Okay, I need you or her to fill out these papers and I will be needing your insurance card."

"Insurance card?" Seven asked.

"Yes, for payment."

"No insurance card, ma. I'm paying cash if you don't mind," Seven answered modestly. Seven pulled out a rubber-banded knot that was full of hundred-dollar bills and placed it on the desk, making the receptionist's eyes almost pop out of her head. Seven never used cards, always cash. That was always a hustler's preferred method of payment. "That should do it, right?" Seven asked as he gave her a small grin, making her blush and turn plum red. Seven grabbed the clipboard and returned to Hazel, who was sitting down in the waiting area. He handed her the clipboard and told her she would have to fill it out before they checked her in. Hazel's hands were shaking as she tried her best to shake off the tremors. Seven knew that she was going through withdrawal and tried not to stare at her hand, making her any more uneasy than she already was. He smiled at her and placed his hand on her shoulder, giving her support in this big step that she was taking. He knew that she had been without heroin for about six days and she was on edge. However, she had only been without the drug for one day. Hazel had managed to "stumble" upon the brick of heroin that Seven had hidden in his cereal box, and every time he would leave to make a run, she would take a little and shoot up behind his back; pinching off a little each time. GiGi had set a trap for Hazel and she fell for it. GiGi wanted to see Hazel's world come crashing down, feeling that Hazel and Seven were too close. Jealousy overwhelmed GiGi and Hazel was secretly her worst enemy. Seven didn't know, but his brick was about ten grams off and that eventually would come back and bite him in the ass.

Hazel felt so bad about what she had done. She kept thinking about how she was huddled up in his bathroom shooting up his dope while he didn't even know about it. He was the only one in her corner, but her addiction made all loyalty go flying out of the window. *I'm so sorry, Seven. But you don't understand,* Hazel thought as she finished up the papers and looked at Seven. *The way he looks at me . . . it's different. He doesn't look at me like I'm a dopefiend.* Although Seven was only keeping his word with Apple, he was giving Hazel more than he would ever understand. He was giving her hope and a support system, something she was lacking all her life.

After thirty minutes of getting checked in and situated, a tall, slim doctor came out to greet Hazel. Dr. Young was his name and he was a specialist in behavioral science and drug rehabilitation. The doctor instructed Seven that Hazel would stay at the faculty from 10:00 to 10:00 every day for eight weeks. Hazel really was ready to shake off the addiction and Seven was proud of her for taking the first step, which was getting help.

"Okay, I will be here at ten o'clock sharp to come get you, ma," Seven stated.

"Okay, thanks," she said just before she hugged him tightly. "Thanks for everything, Seven," she whispered in his ear as they embraced each other.

"Don't mention it. I told you I got you, right?" Seven said as he looked down at her and into her eyes. The doctor shook Seven's hand and lead

Hazel into the back, preparing her for her first step into recovery.

Seven watched as they faded into the back and then he left, ready to hit the streets. He had much business to handle and his first stop was on the south side to hit his man with the brick he had put up for him.

An hour later, Seven was pulling into Regency Apartments, the stomping ground of one of his most faithful buyers: Mouse. Mouse was a hustler who migrated from New York and set up shop in Flint, where his family had already been. Seven pulled out his phone and called Mouse, letting him know he was outside with the brick of heroin for him. Seven parked his truck and cocked his pistol, putting it on the left side of him in the car door's side pocket. Seven didn't trust Mouse too much, but had been doing business with him for years. Mouse had been running the south side's drug market, while Seven ran the north's. Seven was Mouse's supplier and that always gave him the upper hand. Without being said, that made Mouse under Seven on the hustler's totem pole; Mouse hated that. Mouse wanted so bad to have Seven's heroin connect, but that was something Seven would never give up until he was out of the game himself.

Mouse came out of the building with a bubbled down coat and a tight skull cap on his head. His butter-colored Timberland boots added a couple of inches to his short height, which was just under five foot five. Mouse climbed into the car and looked around before he spoke.

"What up, God," Mouse said in his heavy New York accent. Seven nodded his head, acknowledging him. Seven hated meeting Mouse with dope, let alone in his own territory. Seven would usually have Rah or one of his runners make a drug transaction on his behalf. However, Mouse always insisted on dealing with Seven face to face, not wanting to deal with anyone other than the boss. Being that he was a consistent buyer and never copping under a whole brick, Seven gave him the courtesy of dropping the dope off once a month.

"What you got for me?" Mouse asked as he pulled out a brown paper bag from his inside pocket that was full of cash. Seven then reached under his seat and grabbed the Saran-wrapped kilo of dope and handed it to him. Mouse's eyes lit up when he saw the package, which had a stamp of a naked lady on it; Hassan's signature dope called *Lady Luck*. Mouse began to think about how he was about to get money and then he handed Seven the bag full of money. "It's all there," Mouse said assuringly as he examined the brick.

"Better be," Seven said coldly as he put the money under his seat and started up his car, signaling for Mouse to get out. Seven didn't care for Mouse much and he always let it show; never being too friendly because he knew if Mouse could take his spot, he would without hesitation. Seven hit the unlock button as he looked forward, always keeping it short and sweet with him. Mouse looked at Seven, cutting his eye, but he remained silent knowing that he didn't want to ruffle any feathers with his connect.

"I'll call you when I'm ready to re-up," Mouse said as he stepped out of the car, stuffing the brick into his coat. Seven nodded and pulled off, not knowing that he had just shorted his man in product, all because of Hazel's sneakiness and disloyalty.

Look at these crazy-looking mufuckas. I cannot believe I am in here doing this, Hazel thought as she glanced at the strangers in the room with her, who were sitting in plastic school chairs that formed a circle. Everyone in the room was at least twice her age and she was very uncomfortable and felt out of place. She just crossed her arms and watched as she showed little to no emotion.

"Hello, my name is Margaret," the redhead said in her raspy voice. It sounded as if she had been smoking cigarettes since the age of two.

"Hello, Margaret," everyone said in unison, greeting her.

What the fuck? They sound like they're in a damn cult or something. This some bullshit! I do not belong here. Hazel crossed her arms and watched them make fools of themselves. She even began to examine each addict there, picking something out on them that she could make an inside joke about. She wasn't feeling the program at all and figured that she would at least have fun since she had to be there. *Look at this ugly bitch,* Hazel thought, almost bursting out in laughter as she looked at Margaret's crooked red wig that sat on top of her head.

Hazel was the only one in the room who didn't acknowledge her. Dr. Young sat in the middle, mediating and directing the confessional exercise with his notebook and pen in hand.

"And I am a heroin addict," Margaret said proudly as she stood up before everyone. Hazel leaned over and whispered to Dr. Young as Margaret gave her testimonial. "I have to use the restroom."

Dr. Young nodded his head and Hazel slipped out. "Fuck this," Hazel said as she ripped the name tag sticker that was on her shirt. Hazel swiftly grabbed her coat that was on the rack and snuck out of the back entrance on her way as far from Insight Rehabilitation Center as possible. As she stepped onto the main road, she began to get that itch. Her body was just beginning to cry out for her Jones and, instantly, Hazel went into scavenger mode wanting to feel the magic travel up her veins. She began to scratch her itching forearm and became jumpy. The ecstasy of the drug was what she craved insatiably. It grew more and more by the second and her slow, aimless walk turned into a brisk strut on her way to the hood, which was about five miles away. "I need to get up with Millie," she whispered as she headed toward Millie's projects that were a straight shot down the road. She had ten hours to do her thing and come back so Seven could pick her up. Hazel didn't know how, but she was about to get high . . . by any means necessary.

Chapter Nine

The sun was shining, but snow still covered the streets and sidewalks. Hazel finally made it to Millie's apartment complex after a forty-five-minute walk that seemed like an eternity. Her toes were cold and her heart was pounding, hoping that Seven didn't roll up on her while she was out trying to get high rather that at Insight. Hazel made it to Millie's apartment, which had an outside entrance, and knocked, hoping that she was there and not already gone to cop her first shot of the day without her. Hazel knocked on the door again and waited for a response. "Come on, Millie," Hazel whispered as she blew into her hands, trying to warm them. After a minute straight of non-stop knocking, Millie answered the door. She had a rag on her head and a robe on as she opened the door, yawning.

"Hey, baby," she whispered as she walked into the living room and flopped on the couch. Hazel walked in and looked at the apartment, which she had not seen in a week or so.

"Hey, Millie," Hazel said as she walked into the apartment. The apartment was small and tidy, not what you would think a dope addict lived in. Hazel had been living with her up until Seven came and got her. Millie had pretended to be crazy and got some case worker to grant her an SSI check, which worked out great for Millie. On the first of the month she would pay all her bills and shot the rest of the money up in her veins. Hazel sat on the couch and watched as Millie faded into the bathroom.

"You got any?" Hazel yelled back so she could hear her.

"Hell naw! I wish. I thought you did, coming over this early."

Millie yelled as she began to wash her face with the door open, where Hazel could see her.

"Hell naw. I need some bad though. My stomach hurts like a mufucka."

Millie returned to the living room, unwrapped her hair, lit a cigarette, and put a pot of coffee on. "And where the hell you been, Hazelnut? I haven't heard from you in a week. The last time I saw you Seven was dragging yo' ass out of the spot."

"Yeah, that nigga be tripping. After we went to see Apple in jail, he has been on my ass like white on rice. He said he want me to get clean and all,"

Hazel said as she began to hold her stomach as the sharp pain shot through it. "And this nigga got the nerve to try to put me in some rehab place. I took one look at them lames and dipped out. Fuck that."

Millie poured herself a cup of coffee and joined Hazel on the couch. She looked at Hazel and remorse was all she could feel. She was looking at a fiend who was once an innocent little girl. She was the blame for her addiction and it burdened her soul. However, Hazel was on a destructive path anyway if Millie knew it or not. Hazel always was extra curious about heroin. It was only a matter of time before she experimented with it.

"That's not a bad idea, girl. Maybe it is time for you to shake this shit," Millie said, meaning every word of it. Millie put her cigarette in the ashtray and grabbed Hazel by the hands, squeezing them slightly. "I remember the first day I met you. You came in the detention center sweet as pie and look at you know. You a gangster!" Millie said, smiling, trying to get Hazel to smile too. "Naw, but fa' real . . . You should let Seven help you out. I already fucked up my life, but you don't have to do this shit. When I was about your age, a man who I loved so much got me off that shit, but I didn't stay strong and I regret that shit every day," Millie said as she rubbed the tattoo on her neck that read "Tical," the deceased man she was referring to. "When you do them drugs . . . it takes away your soul," Millie said as tears began to form in her eyes. Hazel reminded Millie so much of herself, it was surreal to her.

"I know . . . I know," Hazel said as she dropped her head, knowing Millie was telling her nothing but the truth. Millie talked to Hazel for about an hour, but that "getting clean" conversation quickly ended once Millie began to get her Jones and her stomach also began to call for dope. With two weak-willed addicts and no one contesting their high . . . they left Millie's apartment, searching for their first shot of the day.

Seven sat at his low-key apartment where he and Rah kept their money and most of the product. Only they knew the whereabouts of the place, which was on the east side, about twenty minutes from Seven's territory. The sound of the money machine was like music to Seven's ears. He had just flipped the whole ten bricks that Hassan had hit him with within a week's time. Rah pulled the money out of the book bag and stacked it on the table, preparing them to go through the machine. Seven had made more money in that past week than he had in the last six months. Hassan really put him on another level as far as the dope game was concerned.

In the midst of the money counting process, Seven's phone rang.

"Yo'," Seven said as he put his phone to his ear.

"That's fucked up, my nigga," the man said on the other end of the phone. Seven pulled the phone from his ear and looked at the caller ID to see who was on the other end; it was Mouse from the south side.

"What you talking about?" Seven asked calmly.

"You shorted me on the brick. You owe me about a quarter brick," Mouse lied, really only being short about ten grams.

Mouse had an aggressive tone, obviously irritated by Seven.

"Yo', you betta fall back, homeboy. I weighed them shits up myself. It was on point when I gave it to you. Don't try to pull that slick shit because I ain't for it," Seven said coldly.

"It's like that?" Mouse asked while getting more angry at the situation the more he thought about it. "Somebody coming up with my shit. I ain't taking no shorts!" Mouse screamed into the phone.

"Have a nice day, sir," Seven answered nonchalantly while smirking and pushing the end button at the same time. He looked at Rah and shook his head from side to side. "See, that's why I don't deal with niggas. They always are trying to squeeze you for more, trying to get over. I hate petty niggas."

"Why? Who was that? What happened?" Rah asked while wrapping a rubber band around a stack of money.

"That was Mouse bitch ass," Seven answered.

"From the south side? I never liked that nigga. He grimey as hell. Don't know why you deal with the nigga anyway."

"He spends good money with me. That's the only reason why. But now I'ma cut his ass off. He said that his pack was short, but I sat and watched Natasha weigh up every brick at Hassan's house. Every brick was on point! Clown-ass nigga," Seven said as he continued the money process. They both shook their heads and swept the situation under the rug and chalked it up to the game . . . but Mouse didn't.

Hazel stood outside in the cold as she blew into her hands and shifted from one foot to the other trying to stay warm. "Come on, Millie," Hazel said to herself as she eyed the door to the dope house that Millie had gone in about five minutes before. Hazel gave her the twenty dollars that Seven had given her for lunch so that Millie could buy dope instead. Millie came storming out of the dope house yelling with a frown on her face.

"Fuck y'all then! Y'all scared of money!" Millie said as she walked off the porch to join Hazel.

"What happened?" asked Hazel.

"They won't let me cop because of you. Seven got them shook. I mean . . . nobody wouldn't sell me shit. This some bullshit!" Millie replied, frustrated as hell.

"Fuck! Let's just cop from that spot in Selby Hood," Hazel recommended as she gripped her aching stomach.

"Hell naw. We might as well not cop if we gon' cop that bullshit. We need some of that *Lady Luck*," Millie said as she began to walk down the street thinking hard about where they could go and cop. "Oh, I know!" Millie said excitedly as she stopped in her tracks and smiled. "Last week I copped some good shit from this trick nigga on the south side."

"Shit, let's go," Hazel said, as she didn't want to waste any time. A twenty-minute bus ride to the south side was worth it to get some good dope.

"I think the nigga name was . . . Mouse."

Chapter Ten

Mouse sat in his Lexus that was pulled on the curb, observing his trap spot making money. His goon sat to the right of him in the passenger seat with a notebook on his lap. Three lines of coke were lined up as the goon dipped his head quickly and immediately used his nose as a vacuum, sucking up the first line. He quickly rose up and threw his head back to prevent it from running. He made sniffing noises and wiped his nose clean.

"So what you wanna do about that nigga Seven," the goon asked as his trigger finger began to itch. Mouse had told his crew that Seven had shorted him and then acted like nothing was wrong with doing so. The fact that Seven wasn't trying to make up the shortage of dope made Mouse even more irate. The way that Seven blew him off was a blow to Mouse's pride and that made for chaos.

"The nigga was on some boss shit . . . like he wasn't trying to give me what I paid for. Some nerve! I got him though. I'ma show that nigga what's up," Mouse said confidently and he slowly nodded his head up and down, plotting on revenge. "Do that nigga know who the fuck I am?" Mouse asked rhetorically, getting angrier the more he thought about it as he grabbed the notebook and hit a line. Just as he lifted his head, a knock on the window startled him and he and his goon went for their guns. The woman on the outside knocking couldn't see through the tint so she was squinting her eyes and put her hands against the glass, over her eyes, trying to see if someone was in the running car. Mouse saw who it was and put his gun back onto his waist and his goon followed suit.

"Don't be running up on my shit like that! I almost popped yo' ass," Mouse said as he rolled down his window, slowly exposing his face.

"Chill out, baby boy. My bad," Millie said as she smiled, trying to ease the mood as she stepped away from the car.

"This that bitch I was telling you about," Mouse whispered to his goon as he briefly glanced at him and looked back at Millie. Mouse had been telling him about a dopefiend who had some bomb pussy. The tripped-out part about it was that she didn't even look like a dopefiend, and Mouse found that amusing. A week earlier Millie rode his dick so good, he bust in thirty seconds flat and it only cost him a twenty pack of *Lady Luck*. Mouse had been thinking about her all week and there she was, standing right in front of him looking desperate.

"You got some?" Millie asked as she blew in her hand, trying to stay warm while ducking so that she could be eye level with Mouse.

"You know I keep that," Mouse said arrogantly. "You got some money?" he said, knowing that she didn't.

"Naw, I'm hurting right now, but I got something better than that," Millie said as she ran her tongue over her top lip, trying to entice him.

"Oh, yeah?" Mouse asked while grinning. He already felt his pole growing in his jeans and his mind was on getting another shot of Millie's bomb sex.

"Yep," Millie said as she turned around and let Mouse get a glimpse of her ass that seemed to stay with her regardless of her addiction. The ass was usually the first to go when dealing with drugs, but not Millie's.

Without hesitation, Mouse turned off his car and stepped out. His goon got out too, anticipating a train on Millie. "Yo', let's step in the spot,"

Mouse said as he licked his lips and smacked Millie's ass. He then noticed another girl standing a couple of feet away, obviously waiting on Millie. "She with you?" Mouse asked as he checked her out.

"Yeah, she cool," Millie confirmed. They all headed into one of the apartments that Mouse rented for distribution. Millie and Hazel were happy to be in some heat; they had been outside for more than an hour looking for Mouse's car.

"The more the merrier," Mouse said as he headed into the apartment. Hazel grew uncomfortable because of the way the goon was looking at her. He smacked her ass as they made their way into the spot, which made her feel like the scum of the Earth.

As soon as they entered, Mouse's hands began to grope Millie. "Let's go to the back," he suggested.

"All right, cool," Millie said as she pulled off her coat and began to unbuckle her pants, already knowing the deal. She hated trading sex for drugs, but when heroin called for her, it was a craving like no other. Mouse faded into the back room, sparking a blunt, wanting to get high before he blew Millie's back out.

"Hazelnut, I'll be right back," Millie said as she watched Hazel sit on the couch. The goon was standing by the door, standing a couple of feet away from Hazel.

"Okay," Hazel answered, seeming very uptight. Mouse's goon began to look at Hazel like a lion looked at a piece of meat and his pipe began to grow as he thought about sexing her. Her thick thighs and pretty face had him fantasizing. With his big eyes and big lips he wasn't exactly the ladies' man, so paying for sex wasn't new to him. He was prepared to give Hazel whatever she wanted in exchange for him sliding inside of her.

"So, what you want, ma? Dope, blow . . . money?" he asked as he pulled out a large bundle of heroin and waved it from side to side; Hazel's eyes followed.

"Uh-uh. Don't even think about it, playboy," Millie cut in just before she stepped entirely into the back bedroom where Mouse was waiting. "She doesn't get down. I will take care of you. Just come in the back," Millie said as she stopped in her tracks and walked over to the goon.

"I think she's a big girl. She can talk for herself," the goon said as he didn't take his eyes off of Hazel. He licked his lips and was getting horny. "So what you gon' do?" he asked again, seeing her eyes light up at the sight of the *Lady Luck* he was holding.

"I said . . . I got you. Just come back and get some of this. I can handle the both of you," Millie said, being overprotective of Hazel as she stormed over to the goon and grabbed his dick. Millie began to stroke it while it was growing in his jeans.

"I'm grown. I can handle this," Hazel said as she stood up. She wanted that bag to herself so she wanted to earn it by herself. Millie looked at Hazel as if she was crazy and then pulled the goon toward the back room, but not before Hazel grabbed his hand. "I got this," she said again.

Millie looked at Hazel as an adult and not a little girl. At that moment, she knew that Hazel was not a teen anymore and was about to open Pandora's box. Millie quickly decided to let Hazel take care of her own business, and went into the back with Mouse not wanting to keep him waiting any longer. If Millie was in her right mind and not yearning for the drug so badly, she would have protested more, but the only thing on her mind was making Mouse have a good nut so that he would reward her with a large pack of *Lady Luck*. She left Hazel alone with the goon and went into the back.

"Handle this for me, ma," the goon said as he pulled out his slightly erect penis. Hazel's heart was beating so fast and hard, it seemed as if she had a baboon inside of her chest trying to get out. Hazel walked over to him, dropped on her knees, and closed her eyes.

What the hell am I doing? I'm just like my damn mama, she thought as she froze for a second. Just as she thought about getting up and backing out, the pains in her stomach reminded her who the boss was. She was a slave to her own addiction and it seemed like an out-of-body experience as she took him into her mouth and began sucking, only thinking about the high that she would experience afterward. Tears streamed down her face as she let him thrust into her mouth while grabbing her hair roughly, not caring about how he treated her. Hazel had just crossed a line that she had promised herself she would never.

Thirty minutes had passed and Millie came out of the back room, followed by the smell of sex and weed, to find Hazel waiting on the couch anxiously. Hazel was waiting so she and Millie could go and shoot the dope up together. Hazel had only had the dope for fifteen minutes but in dopefiend time it was an eternity.

"Damn, Millie, you took long enough! Let's go," Hazel said as she had her coat on, ready to leave. The goon was in the corner sitting in the chair, while smoking a Newport cigarette, feeling good off the orgasm that he had just had in Hazel's mouth. Mouse came out seconds later, buttoning up his jeans, also feeling good. Millie had just ridden his pipe like an award-winning cowgirl and she earned every bit of the dope he had just given her.

"Okay, we out," Millie said as she headed to the door. Millie and Hazel stepped outside and the cold air hit them like a bus. Chills ran up both of their bodies as they both dipped their heads into the coats.

"You know any spots on this side of town?" Hazel asked, not trying to wait until they reached Millie's house to shoot up.

"Hell naw. Damn!" Millie said, feeling the same urgency as Hazel was. Mille began to look around, trying to think of a place they could go. "Wait, yeah I do! It's a spot around the way. The only thing is, I don't really know homeboy like that. But he has a shooting gallery in his basement. He charges five dollars at the door." Millie said, using a nickname fiends gave houses that people shot their dope at. "I went there awhile back, but it's nasty as hell in there," Millie said, sounding like she didn't want to go.

"So, fuck it, let's go there. We need somewhere warm where we can get high. Your house is at least thirty, forty minutes away. We will leave right after we done," Hazel said, anxiously trying to hurry to her first shot of the day.

Ten minutes had passed and Millie and Hazel were at the back door at the spot anxiously waiting to get in. Millie knocked on the door and then rubbed her hands together, trying to keep warm. "These mufuckas need to hurry up. It's colder than a bitch out here."

"Who dat?" a man's voice yelled from the inside.

"*Lady Luck,*" Millie yelled back, giving him the code word to let him know what she was coming to do. The sounds of locks being clicked and then a chain being slid sounded. The door opened and an older man with spaced-out teeth stood before them.

"Ten dollars," he said as he held his palm out and wiggled his fingers. Millie dug into her bra and pulled out a crumpled-up ten-dollar bill that she had gotten from Mouse. She put it in the man's hand and the man stepped aside, giving them a path to enter the dope house. Hazel followed Millie into the dark house and they walked down the creaky steps that lead to the basement. The big basement was dimly lit with a jukebox that sat in the corner, giving it a look of a 1970s speakeasy. There was a mixed crowd of men and women as they were in various places shooting their dope. The jukebox played a slow melody by Marvin Gaye, and Hazel felt like she was in an old-time movie. Everyone was cool and laidback as they bobbed their heads to the tunes. Millie quickly found a table that sat in the corner and began to do their thing. The first shot was always the best. Hazel quickly got comfortable and she let Millie set up as she took her coat off and hurriedly rolled up her sleeve. "This is about to feel so good," she whispered as she watched Millie fill the syringe.

Chapter Eleven

Hazel woke up and quickly wiped the slobber that dribbled from the corner of her mouth. She looked over at Millie who was sitting in the chair, nodding, slowly letting her chin touch her chest, just before she quickly popped back up, trying to keep herself from falling.

"Millie . . . Millie," Hazel whispered harshly as she watched Millie pop up for the second time. Millie still had her eyes closed, so Hazel pulled her arm, finally waking her.

"Hey, Hazelnut," Millie mumbled as she barely opened her eyes and looked at Hazel with a smile. Millie had shot up twice the amount of Hazel, so she was twice as high off *Lady Luck*.

"Let's go . . . I got to get back to the rehab center," Hazel said, not knowing how long she had been nodding. Hazel looked around the room and noticed that it had cleared out and they were the only two left down there. "Millie!" Hazel yelled, nervous about what time it was.

She didn't want Seven to come pick her up at Insight and she wasn't there. Millie slowly came to and began to lick her chapped lips. Millie glanced at her wristwatch and then took a deep breath.

"Relax, Hazelnut, its only two o'clock," Millie confirmed as she sat up from her slouched position.

"Oh," Hazel said as she relaxed, knowing that she had plenty of time to get back. "You got some more?" Hazel asked, not remembering how much they had used earlier.

"Yeah, I got about a tenth left," Millie confirmed, which was more than enough to have them leaning for the rest of the evening. All of a sudden, the sound of someone moving in the corner of the room echoed throughout the basement. Millie and Hazel's eyes shot over to the dark corner and they saw a man sitting there who was just waking from a nod. He still had the needle in his arm and a belt wrapped tightly around his forearm.

"Can I hit that with y'all?" he asked after overhearing what Millie said about her having a tenth left. Millie instantly smacked her lips and rolled her eyes, not giving the man a second thought.

"Negro, please!" she said as she whipped out the bag with the *Lady Luck* symbol stamped on it. Hazel's eyes instantly followed the bag as she anticipated hitting it again. Hazel picked up the syringe while feeling her heart pound as her adrenaline began to pump. Millie and Hazel both were so focused on setting up, they didn't see the six-foot three man stand up and approach them while they sat at the table.

"Is that *Lady Luck*?" he asked as he hovered over them. He could smell the strong vinegar aroma from where he was standing and he knew that it was the best thing Flint had to offer as far as dope was concerned. He wanted in.

"Uh-uh, homeboy! You betta back the fuck up!" Millie said as she looked up and snapped her neck back, not believing that the man was all in their business. Hazel's eyes were on the dope, so she never saw the surprise coming. The man struck Millie square in the eye, causing her to fly out of the chair.

"Millie," Hazel screamed as she watched her hold her eye and ball up into fetal position. The man was crazed and in need of dope, so he decided he would take what Millie wasn't trying to share. The man repeatedly began to kick Millie in the midsection, catching her square in her stomach with every blow. It seemed as if Hazel's high had instantly been ripped from her and the feeling of fear overcame her. Hazel immediately rose up and lunged onto the man's back while scratching and biting him.

"Get the hell off of her!" Hazel demanded as she held on for dear life.

"Aghhh! Bitch!" the man yelled in pain as he twisted wildly, trying to get a feisty Hazel off of his back. He staggered backward, reached over his shoulder, and grabbed Hazel's hair violently. He got a good grip and flung her across the room with all his brute strength, making her bump her head violently on the hard, cement floor. He then grabbed the dope off of the table, but Millie wasn't giving up her dope that easy. She whipped out a switchblade knife that she always kept in her bra, flicked it open, and stabbed the man in his foot with all of her might as he tried to gather the heroin off of the table.

"You li'l bitch!" the man screamed as he watched Millie raise her hand again, attempting to give him another stab. But before she could poke him, he kicked the knife out of her hand, causing it to skid across the floor near Hazel who was on all fours trying to regain her focus. The man began to beat Millie, giving her punch after punch to the face and her body. Millie couldn't defend herself and began blacking out because of the man's violent rampage on her. Hazel grabbed the knife and ran up on the man, and without even thinking twice she plunged the knife into the side of his neck with all of her might, causing blood to shoot out instantaneously. The man, right away, grabbed his neck and began to gasp for air. Hazel, crying hysterically, watched as the man fell over and onto his back as he struggled to breathe. Blood oozed from his mouth and his eyes began to roll into the back of his head.

Hazel knelt down and propped up Millie's head as she was fading in and out of consciousness. "Millie . . . Millie," Hazel cried. Moments later, the man who originally let them in came down the stairs to see what all of the commotion was about.

"What the hell is going . . ." he started to ask just before he stopped mid-sentence. He saw the battered women and his get-high buddy laid out on the floor in his own blood. "Oh my God," he whispered as he put his hand over his mouth and looked on in disbelief.

Millie began to come to and looked over at the man who was lying there dead with his eyes wide open and a knife sticking out the side of his neck. She sat up and asked Hazel if she was okay. Hazel was crying so hard that she couldn't talk. She just nodded her head and she stood on her knees, rocking back and forth. Millie crawled over to the man and spit in his face boldly as she took the dope that was balled up in his hands.

"What the fuck have y'all done?" the man asked as he sat down on the steps and put his hands on his head. "I already got two strikes! I can't deal with this shit. Y'all bitches got to get this nigga outta here! This some crazy shit right here," he admitted as he shook his head from side to side, not believing what had just happened in the basement of his own house.

Hazel didn't know what to do. She looked to Millie, but she was still disoriented from the attack. Hazel only had one option. She had to call Seven. "Where's the phone?" Hazel asked the man as she began to wipe her tears away.

About an hour later Seven and Ra were walking into the house, Rah having a chrome nine millimeter in his hand. "Lock that door," Seven ordered to Rah as he stepped in and looked around, scanning the entire room.

"We're down here!" the man yelled from the basement. Seven had gotten a call from Hazel and immediately went to her. Seven looked around suspiciously to locate where the voice was coming from. The man repeated himself but that time louder, and then Seven and Rah followed the voice that led them to the basement.

Seven slowly walked down the basement stairs, followed closely by Rah. When he reached the bottom step, the familiar smell of heroin and the stink stench of the basement invaded his nostrils. The first thing Seven saw was the dead body on the floor. He then looked at Hazel, Millie, and the man who the house belonged to, standing over the body. Hazel was crying when she had called Seven, so he didn't know the extent of the problem. She refused to tell him over the phone and begged him to come to the house. After giving him the address, he headed over.

"What the fuck?" Seven whispered as he stared at the dead body.

"Seven!" Hazel said as she ran into his arms, sobbing. "I didn't mean to do it! He . . . he was hurting Millie," she cried as she broke down into his arms.

"Calm down. Calm down, ma," Seven whispered into her ear as he embraced her tightly. Hazel took his words in heed and calmed down. Seven grabbed her by her shoulders and looked her into her watery eyes. With his piercing eyes and cold stare, he demanded, "Tell me exactly what happened, Hazel. From beginning to end. Don't leave out anything."

Millie immediately cut in, loud and asserting, while holding a pack of frozen vegetables on the side of her face to keep the swelling down. "Me and Hazel were down here minding our own damn—" Millie said, but Seven raised his hand, signaling her to stop talking, and gave her a look that could kill. The look was so menacing, so sinister, so sincere that Millie instantly closed her mouth and smacked her lips.

"I asked Hazel!" he said, while raising his tone, something that he rarely did.

"We were down here getting high . . . and he just came over and tried to rob us of the dope we had. He started to beat Millie and . . ." She started to breath heavily. "And I stabbed him. I killed him, Seven. I'm so sorry. I know I should have stayed at Insight. I'm so sorry," she said as she dropped her head and cried while shaking her head from side to side.

"Anybody see what happened?" Seven asked, knowing just how to solve the problem accordingly.

"No, just Mille and me were down here," Hazel said as she looked at Seven.

"Are you sure?" he asked again.

"I'm positive. Only person knows about it is him. He came down right after it went down," Hazel answered. That's all Seven had to hear. He looked back at Rah and winked at him, giving him the signal. Without hesitation Rah stepped over the dead body, standing right in front of the man, and pointed his gun to his head. The man didn't even have a chance to say anything in his own defense. Boom! Rah rocked him to sleep, giving him a hollow-tip bullet straight through his forehead, making him drop immediately. He was dead before he even hit the floor. Millie and Hazel both jumped at the sound of the unexpected gunshot. Blood splattered on Millie's face because she was standing next to him. She dropped her bag of vegetables and her knees began to tremble in fear. Her ears started to ring and she couldn't hear out of her left ear momentarily.

"What the fuck!" Millie asked as her eyes grew big as golf balls.

"Oh my God!" Hazel yelled as she clung to Seven.

"No witnesses, no murder," Seven whispered to Hazel, explaining the rules of the game to her in very few words. Rah then pointed the gun to Millie's head.

"What about her?" Rah asked as Millie was standing there frozen with fear while looking down the barrel of Rah's gun.

"Oh, it's like that, playboy?" Millie said without any fear in her heart. "How I look?" Millie said as she fixed her hair, being her same self even in the face of death.

"Nooo!" Hazel screamed as she looked at Rah and then back at Seven. Seven paused, deciding what he was going to do about Millie, who could potentially tell someone what had happened that day.

"Seven! No!" Hazel said as she grabbed Seven's collar.

"Rah, leave her alone . . . for now," Seven said coldly as he gently pulled Hazel's grip from his cotton polo shirt.

Rah gave Millie a small smirk and then he lowered his gun, putting it in the front pocket of his hoodie. Rah then pulled out a handkerchief and began to wipe the blood that had also splattered on his face. Seven walked over to Millie and swiftly put his hand around her neck and squeezed so tightly that she couldn't get any oxygen. Hazel wanted to tell him to stop, but the look in his eyes told a story of its own. *Don't fuck with me,* was what they said, and Hazel just sat back and watched.

"Listen and listen close. I am only going to say this once. Stay . . . away . . . from . . . Hazel," he said through his clenched teeth as he tightened his grip, causing veins to form in his hands. "If I catch you around her again, I will kill you. You can take that to the bank," he said, sincerely meaning every word that escaped his mouth.

"Okay," Millie managed to say as she stood on her tippy toes, slightly lifting her body off the ground. Just barely, Millie managed to whisper "Okay." Seven released his grip and let Millie fall to her knees while holding her neck, trying to catch her breath.

"Let's get the fuck out of here," Seven added as he shook his head from side to side in disappointment. Seven turned around and left, grabbing Hazel by the arm, making her go with him. Hazel wanted to stay with Millie, but she understood that her way of living would eventually land her in one of two places: dead or in jail. That day was her wake-up call. Hazel looked back at Millie and watched as she tried to catch her breath. It was painful knowing that she had to leave her, breaking their bond, but she knew it had to be done for her to get well. She was about to play by Seven's rules and try to change her life. She decided that right then and there, she was about to give a change for Apple, for Seven, and most important . . . for herself.

Chapter Twelve

Week One of Recovery

Seven sat in the corner of the meeting room reading a book while frequently glancing over at Hazel. He observed her as she frantically scratched herself while clenching her jaws tightly. She sat in a discussion circle along with the other recovering addicts in the rehab center. Seven had decided to stay with her throughout the healing process and wouldn't leave her side until she was drug-free. He had put Rah in charge of his drug business and took a brief hiatus to give his undivided attention to Hazel's recovery.

Hazel hated the fact that Seven was with her around the clock because it prevented her from falling off the wagon and going back to the drugs that she wanted—no, needed so badly. She looked around at the addicts giving their testimonies and it made her sick to her stomach knowing that she was in the same boat as those strung-out people. She wished Millie were there with her; at least they could make jokes and laugh at the people there. But Millie was in a place unknown and Hazel was there alone, battling her own demons. Seven was her only crutch. Hazel had had enough and got up, excusing herself from the group. However, Seven got up right with her with his arms crossed, giving her a stern look. Almost immediately, Hazel stopped in her tracks, smacked her lips, and turned around, returning to the circle. Seven was about to be on her like white on rice and this was only the beginning.

Week Three of Recovery

Seven sat at the end of the bed, rubbing Hazel's sweaty back as she tossed and turned in her sleep fighting the demons that withdrawal had to offer. The sounds of thunder and rain hitting the windowpane serenaded the night's woes. Seven was there every step of the way, trying to get Hazel off heroin. She scratched herself in her sleep and occasionally woke up sweaty and paranoid, but Seven was there every time to let her know that everything was okay.

"Everything is going to be okay. I got you," he whispered. At first Seven was helping Hazel solely because of the fact of who her father was. But somewhere along the line . . . he began to help her because he wanted to. Hazel and Seven, throughout her recovery, became more than friends.

Week Eight of Recovery

It had been two months since Seven dedicated himself to getting Hazel clean and all the hard work had paid off. Seven was in the front row dressed in a designer slacks and a crisp, tan dress shirt, with a beige and cream tie. Rather than the biggest dope man in Flint, he looked like he stepped right off the pages of *GQ* magazine with his business attire. It was a special occasion, so he stepped out of his usual realm for Hazel, dressing accordingly. He watched as Hazel stood in line, preparing to get her certificate of completion from Insight. She had been drug-free for sixty days and Seven had been with her every step of the journey. It had been a hard one, but they made it together. *Hazel is a beautiful woman,* Seven thought as he couldn't take his eyes off of her. It was hard to see that through the glaze in her eyes that the heroin caused, but now they were clear and Seven was taking notice of the real Hazel. He watched her stand in line, frequently looking at him and grinning from ear to ear.

"Hazel Brown," Dr. Young said into the microphone as he looked to his left and smiled at Hazel, who seemed more vibrant than ever. She no longer had dark circles around her eyes and she had a certain glow about her that somehow got lost while she was doing the dope.

Seven stood up and joined the auditorium in congratulating her for the remarkable achievement. Hazel had become the darling of the rehab center, because she was the youngest and everyone was rooting for her to get clean. She had become everyone's baby and with that, she gained a family that she never had.

Seven gave a rare smile and Hazel glanced down at him from the stage and returned the smile, almost dropping a tear; a tear of joy. She walked over and got her certificate and embraced Dr. Young.

"You did it, Hazel. I knew you could. This is only the first step. Now the real challenge begins. But, I know you can do it. You have a strong support system behind you," Dr. Young said as he looked at Seven, who was still standing and clapping slowly.

Thank you so much, Dr. Young," Hazel said while smiling ear to ear, displaying her beautiful, youthful smile.

Hazel took her award and ran off stage, while Dr. Young called another recipient's name on the microphone.

"I'm proud of you, ma," Seven said as Hazel ran into his arms. He hugged her closely, wrapping his strong arms around her body, letting her know she was safe and secure with him. Hazel closed her eyes and rested her head on his chest, smelling the clean scent of his cologne.

"Let's get out of here. I have a surprise for you," Seven said as he threw his arm around her shoulders.

"A surprise?" Hazel asked as she looked up at him and gave him a skeptical smirk.

"Come on, I will show you," Seven said calmly as the smile left his face and he threw his head in the direction of the exit. Hazel was excited to see what Seven had for her. She hadn't had anyone surprise her with anything since the absence of her father. Hazel and Seven walked down the aisle, heading out. Hazel was so excited, she never noticed Millie, who sat in the back row with tears in her eyes. Millie had been staying away from Hazel, knowing that it would be best for her. Millie watched her "Hazelnut" get her award and it made her so happy. She had finally gotten some sort redemption for introducing Hazel to heroin. Millie's heart fluttered as she watched Hazel leave the auditorium with Seven. Hazel was the only family she had. To know that she was clean it made her horrible world seem better just for a brief moment. "I love you, baby," Millie whispered as she watched Hazel exit with Seven's arm around her. Her pride and joy had just walked out of the door. Millie hadn't realized how much she needed Hazel until she had been out of her life. Millie got inspired to get clean just like Hazel had done, but reality quickly sat back in when her Jones came a-knocking. Millie felt the familiar sharp pain shoot through her stomach. She stuck her hand inside her jacket's pocket to make sure her dope packet and needle were still there. She gave Hazel and Seven enough time to leave the parking lot and she exited, heading to a shooting gallery so that she could get her first shot of the day.

Chapter Thirteen

Hazel walked with both hands in front of her, trying not to bump into anything. Seven's tie was wrapped around her face, covering her eyes. Seven had pulled into the Benz dealership and was about to give Hazel the surprise that he was referring to earlier that day. Seven guided her as they approached the ocean blue, drop-top convertible that had Hazel's name engraved in the headrest.

"You ready?" Seven asked as they stood right in front of the bumper of the car.

"Yeah, I'm ready," Hazel said while smiling, feeling her heart beat rapidly inside of her chest. Seven untied the tie from her face and Hazel opened her eyes. When she saw the luxury, shiny car her mouth dropped. She quickly turned to Seven.

"Stop bullshitting! This is mine?" she asked as she slightly bounced up and down.

"No bullshit, ma. This yours," Seven said as he reached into his pocket and pulled out the keyless key with the big Mercedes sign on it.

Hazel quickly hugged Seven wildly and stood on her tippy toes to peck him on the cheek.

"Thanks, Da—" Hazel quickly stopped herself just before she accidently called Seven "Daddy" because of the familiarity of the feeling that Apple once had given her. "I mean . . . thanks, Seven," Hazel said, correcting herself. Seven smiled, knowing what she almost called him. He quickly wiped the smile off of his face, not wanting her to know he liked the idea.

"You're welcome. You deserve it," he answered. "Let's test this bad boy out. After you," he said as he handed her the keys. Hazel quickly grabbed them and jumped into the car without opening a door. Seven followed suit and got in right after her. He didn't have to worry about paying the dealer because earlier that morning he hit the chief dealer with $50,000 cash for the car. Without hesitation Hazel started up the car, and the engine purred silently but with power and torque. Seven never even bothered to ask if Hazel had a driver's license, but he soon would find out how she drove. She hit the gas and the sound of tires screeching was the only thing to be heard in the parking lot on the Friday afternoon. "Whoooo!" Hazel yelled as she sped off, feeling free as a bird as her hair blew in the wind.

After thirty minutes of tearing up the highway, Hazel was pulling into Seven's apartment complex.

"Seven, I really appreciate what you do for me," Hazel said as she put her car in park and positioned herself where she was facing him directly. "You made me get clean. I can finally look myself in the mirror and see a soul. For so many years there was nothing there. I look at life so much differently now. That shit doesn't have a hold on me and I owe it all to you. Thank you, Seven. I know I haven't told you this but . . . I love you," Hazel said as a tear flowed down her cheek and dripped off her chin.

Seven paused and let Hazel's words soak in. He wanted to tell her he loved her back, but there was something that stopped him. He had never told anyone that he loved them besides Apple and his own grandmother, so he took those strong words very seriously. He placed his hand on Hazel's inner thigh and rubbed gently. He didn't tell Hazel he loved her back, but his eyes did it for him. Hazel spoke again.

"I promise, when I get a job, I will find a place of my own," Hazel said, knowing that Seven had helped her enough by providing a roof over her head throughout her recovery.

"You know . . . I was thinking maybe you can stick around for a while. I like the way you keep the spot clean for me," he said, giving her a lame excuse to make her stay a little bit longer. Seven didn't want to admit it, but he liked Hazel being around.

Hazel smiled, knowing that Seven didn't want her to leave, and played along. "Okay, I will keep that pigsty clean for you," she said playfully as she placed her hand on top of his.

"Listen, I'm going on a boat trip this summer. Have you ever been on a boat?" Seven asked as he tried to change the mood, not wanting to have a romantic moment with Hazel, out of respect for Apple.

"No, never been. Daddy said he was going to take me on one when I was little . . . but it never happened," Hazel replied.

"Well, a friend of mines takes trips every year and he invited me. I want to go. You game?" Seven asked.

"Yes, I would love that, Seven," Hazel answered, feeling honored that he asked her. Hazel was determined to make Seven her man. She didn't realize, but Seven was her first crush. Her life had been filled with so much strife and drug abuse, she never had the experience of having a crush on a boy nor man. Subsequently, her first love was heroin.

Millie swayed back and forth while smoking a cigarette, waiting in line at the Plasma Center on Pierson Road. It was a center that bought blood for medical use, which was a way to get quick cash. The line was long, filled with heroin users looking to get quick money so they could cop their fix. Millie peeked to the front of the line and smacked her lips, seeing that she was the twentieth person in line.

"They need to hurry the fuck up," Millie whispered to herself as she began to grow impatient, feeling her stomach beginning to rumble. It was the end of the month, so she was strapped for cash. She was on her menstrual cycle, so she couldn't turn a trick to support her habit. Giving blood was her only other option to get a quick buck to cop her dope. Her time was running out and she knew that within the next hour, if she didn't get her dope, she would be balled up in agonizing pain craving it. "Come on," she said as she puffed her cigarette and grew more edgy by the moment. She was jittery and irritated to the max. Millie looked to the front of the line and saw Thelma, a known junkie from the neighborhood. Millie, being an opportunist, quickly got a good idea to get herself to the front of the line. Millie stepped out of the line and went toward Thelma, who had on a wig and shades.

"Thelma," Millie whispered as she tugged the woman's coat. Thelma quickly turned around and looked back at Millie.

"You got the wrong person, honey," Thelma answered, and looked away when she saw who it was. Millie stepped closer to Thelma, invading her personal space.

"Bitch, don't play with me. You betta let me cut or I'ma bust your ass out," Millie whispered as she leaned into Thelma's ear. Millie knew that Thelma had HIV, as well as the whole neighborhood. That was a red flag at the Plasma Center and a sure way to get rejected from the nurses inside. Once you were on record for having infected blood, you were banned from the center and your name placed on a blacklist. Millie knew that Thelma must have had a fake ID and was trying to slip in between the cracks. Thelma had put a faulty disguise, trying to swindle her twenty dollars from the Plasma Center. She couldn't fool Millie though. Millie was about to take full advantage of the situation.

"Look, bitch, you know your name is on that list in there. If they find out who you really are, you ain't getting any money" Millie whispered.

"They ain't going to find out. I got my sister's ID," Thelma muttered, finally looking at Millie, obviously aggravated.

"If I tell them, they would know," Millie said, smiling but meaning every word.

"You wouldn't," Thelma said in a harsh whisper, calling Millie out on her bluff.

"Bitch, try me," Millie said as she stepped back and crossed her arms. "Excuse me!" Millie yelled as she raised her hand while looking toward the front door where the nurse was standing with a clipboard.

"Okay, chill," Thelma said in a harsh whisper as she grabbed Millie's arm. "What do you want from me? Why you hating?'

"Just let me cut. If I don't get my medicine soon, I'ma be fucked up," Millie said as she gripped her stomach, feeling a sharp pain shoot through it as soon as she mentioned it. "And if you let me cut, I'll even share my pack with you," Millie negotiated.

Thelma didn't want to let Millie cut because if they got caught, they both would get kicked out of the line and no one would be getting anything.

"Hurry up," Thelma said as she looked at the nurse about three people ahead of her. Thelma stepped back, giving Millie room to squeeze in.

"Bet," Millie said as she slid in swiftly.

"Hey, you can't cut!" a male fiend said from the back of the line as he thought about how Millie was making his wait longer.

"Shut up, nigga! She was holding my spot for me!" Millie said as she quickly snapped back at him. Millie smiled as she noticed she only had two more people in front of her. Her slick move had just cut her wait time by at least thirty minutes.

"You a dirty bitch," Thelma mumbled as she stood behind Millie and shook her head.

"No, get it right, boo-boo. I'm a bad bitch. I'm ahead of you, ain't I?" Millie said arrogantly as she smiled from ear to ear and took a pull of her cigarette.

Twenty minutes later, Millie was walking out of the center with a crisp twenty-dollar bill. She saw Thelma outside, obviously waiting on her.

"Yo, Millie. They knew who I was and kicked me out. You said you would share your pack with me if I let you cut," Thelma reminded her.

"Well, I changed my mind. Peace!" Millie said as she walked right past her and held two fingers up, leaving Thelma standing there looking dumbfounded. Millie chuckled as she headed to the hood to cop her first shot of the day.

Millie sat inside of her home as she slumped on her sofa with a needle in her arm. She had just used the money from the Plasma Center to get right and *Lady Luck* had her feeling lovely. Just before she drifted off, she saw Hazel's gorgeous smile and visualized how pretty Hazel was at the Insight ceremony. She then thought about how she once had a man that cared for her, like Seven did for Hazel. She thought back to a time where she had a chance to kick her habit and take advantage of having a good man to guide her. However, like most fiends . . . she fucked it up.

***

Sixteen Years Earlier

"Yeah, you black bitch. Squeeze my ass," the white trucker crooned as he furiously pounded the young girl's womb, who lay on this cot in the back of his truck. His 280-pound body continuously landed on the young girl as he continued to call her racial slurs. Millie closed her eyes and moaned, faking she was enjoying the small red penis that went in and out of her.

He needs to hurry up, *Millie thought as she momentarily opened her eyes and saw the man's mouth wide open as drool threatened to fall. She closed her eyes and gripped his sweaty butt as he felt his orgasm approaching. He began to pump faster and faster, until he finally exploded into the condom. He grunted and gave her one last deep thrust before he rolled over and off of Millie. Millie quickly sat up and began to put on her clothes that were on the side of the cot. She wanted to get out of the awful smelling truck, so she could get back to her post and make more money. Once she got fully clothed she looked at the man who panted heavily and stared into space as if he was in a dream.*

"Run it, big daddy," Millie demanded as she held out her hand and began moving her fingers, signaling for him to pay up. He reached into his

boot and pulled out a wad of money. He peeled off a fifty-dollar bill and tossed it to Millie.

"There you go, sunshine," he said as he stuffed his money back into his boot.

"Thanks, honey," Millie said with a big smile. She rubbed the man's limp penis and stood up. She straightened up her clothes and licked her lips sexily. She put the fifty-dollar bill into her purse and closed it.

"So when am I going to see you again, baby? You got some good dick," she lied as she tried to stroke his ego. The man, still on his back and naked, stared at her and smiled as she gave him self-assurance about his subpar performance.

"Well, I have to drop off a shipment to North Carolina and I should be heading back this way in a week or so," he said as he sat up and slipped on his grungy white briefs.

"Well, I'll be right here waiting for you, big boy," Millie said, egging him on.

"You're always at this truck stop?" he asked, thinking about how he would stop on his way back, so that he could get another shot of the sweet thing he just pounded. The truck stop was in a huge parking that also had a diner that had frequent traffic from truckers from all around the country.

"Yep, just about every day! I will be waiting for you, too. It's hard to find a good fuck in this business, ya know?" she said as she watched him eat up every word she said. She had him, putty in her hands. "Well, I'm about to get out of here. You have a safe trip and make sure you stop and see me on your way back." Millie said as she began to walk backward, sexily heading to the front cab of the truck. She tripped over his big boots that sat in the middle of the floor and fell onto the floor. Millie quickly grew an embarrassed look on her face and she scrambled to pick up her purse that she dropped.

"Are you okay?" the John asked as a look of concern washed over his face.

"Whew! Yeah, I'm okay," Millie said as she moved the boots out of her way and got back up. "That was humiliating," she said as she smugly smiled and then headed out. "Come back and see me now!" she instructed just before she stepped out of the truck, leaving him in the back, thinking he was Mandingo or something.

"I sure will, honey," he shouted cockily from the back. Millie stepped out of the truck and hurried to the rest stop. She looked down at the wad of money in her hands that she had just lifted from his boot as she smiled. She flipped through the fifties and twenties and knew that she had hit a jackpot.

"Hell yeah, this looks about . . ." she whispered as she flipped through the bills and continued to

walk briskly toward the diner just a few hundred
feet from her, "five hundred dollars," she said,
finishing her sentence. She kept looking back at
the truck she had just left, hoping that she would
have time to get away before he discovered that
he had just gotten robbed. Although Millie was
only seventeen, she had the wits and savvy of a
full-grown woman. Just looking at her, no one
would guess that she was underage. Her body
was plump in all the right places and the way she
conducted herself was that of a seasoned veteran.
She had been on the streets since she was fifteen
years old and working for her stepfather/pimp
ever since she started to grow breasts. He was
her mother's husband and had been in the pimp-
ing game for years. Millie's mother had fallen
victim to drugs and overdosed when Millie was
only twelve years of age. Millie quickly began to
see her stepfather's true colors after her mother
passed. It didn't take long for her stepfather to
introduce her to the family business.

She was close to the diner and she looked back
one more time to make sure he wasn't coming for
her and the coast was clear. Once she didn't see
him, she pushed open the doors and took a deep
breath. The only thing on her mind was getting to
the dealer who posted in the back of the diner so
that she could cop her fix. She knew that she only
had a few minutes before her stepfather pulled

up and checked up on her. She also had to worry about the trucker finding out what she had done to him and coming for her. But she was so worried about getting high, she wasn't thinking clearly. The only thing on her mind was the warm sensation of heroin crawling up her vein and giving her a dopefiend lean. Her growing heroin habit was a vice that her stepfather introduced her to, just months before. She loved the way it made her feel and it seemed like when she was high off the drug, her pain went away momentarily. When the magic of the drug entered her veins it made her feel invincible and without a care in the world; just the way she thought life should be. She saw the dark-skinned guy with a baseball cap on, sitting in the back of the diner as he always did. She hurried over to him, overanxious as she peeled off a twenty-dollar bill from the wad she had just lifted. She walked over to him and sat across from him as he casually read a newspaper. Millie cleared her throat to get his attention as he acted as if no one was in front of him.

"How much?" he said as he kept his eyes on the paper, not even glancing at her.

"A twenty pack," she said as she looked at the door, hoping that the John wouldn't come in.

"You know you're too young to be fucking with this shit," he said as he shook his head from side to side.

"Nigga, quit with the bullshit. You want this money or not?" she asked, growing irritated with his newfound concern for her. She had copped from him dozens of time and he was picking the wrong time to contest her drug habit. "So nigga, do you?" she questioned as she pushed it toward him. The man finally looked up and then he scanned the room. He folded his newspaper and set it on top of the money. He discreetly picked up the money from under the paper and stuffed it in his pocket. He then put his hands on his lap and so did Millie. He gave her the small baggy under the table and out of sight to anyone. Millie smiled and gripped the bag tightly as she headed out the back door and into the Porta Potty that sat at the back of the place, her "get-high spot." Cloud nine had Millie's name written all over it.

Tical sat in the pickup truck as he scanned the parking lot. He glanced at his clock and sucked his teeth. "Where this dude at?" he said as he leaned back in the seat. He had been waiting for thirty minutes for his connect to meet him at the truck stop. Tical had $60,000 in the bag next to him so that he could buy three kilos of coke. He sat in a black S-10 truck that had piles of haystacks in the back bed of the truck. He tried his best to look like a farmer as he wore a bucket fishing hat and plaid shirt. He had laced the haystacks with pepper, so that it threw off potential police dogs from detection. He planned on stuffing the coke into precut compartments in the haystacks, so he could return back to B-more undetected. "That's why I don't like fucking with this New York nigga," Tical said to himself as he saw a young, dark-skinned girl hurry past his car and head into the diner. Tical was just about ready to leave because his plug was taking so long and that's when he saw his man pull up in a red Lexus with black tint. Tical instantly knew that it was his connect, Red. "This nigga stupid!" he said as he regretted doing business with him. He hated the fact that Red had the audacity to bring a flashy car to their exchange. Tical watched as the car parked and he grabbed the bag and stepped out of the car. He headed over to Red while looking around to peep his surroundings. He saw a heavy-set man with trucker attire yelling obscenities as he stepped out of his eighteen-wheeler. The trucker's eyes danced around the parking lot like he was searching for someone. Tical quickly focused his attention back on Red's car as he approached the car. He opened the door and the loud sounds of Tupac blasted from Red's speakers. Tical quickly turned the volume down as he regretted dealing with Red once again.

"What's up, Baltimore," Red said as he extended his hand for a shake.

"Man, you got the shit?" Tical said coldly as he left Red's hand hanging in the air.

"Man, what's wrong with you today?" Red said as he slowly took his hand back.

"Nothing. So where the shit?" Tical asked again. Red reached in his backseat and grabbed a book bag and set it on his lap.

"I got you together right here. You got the cash?" he asked. Tical and Red exchanged bags and both of them looked at the contents of their bags. Tical dipped his pinky in the Ziploc bag and ran it across his gums. Moments later, his gums began to numb and he knew that Red had hit him with some good product once again.

"I'm out," Tical said as he watched Red thumb through the money.

"So quick?" Red asked as he kept his eyes on the money. Tical didn't answer as he opened the door preparing to get out. Tical stopped just before he exited the car and looked at Red. "Let me say this, and I'm only going to say it once you stupid mufucka. Never drive this car when you dealing with me on business. You moving like you an amateur a' something," Tical said as he slammed the door and didn't give Red the chance to answer. Tical headed into the diner to use the bathroom before he headed back home.

Red wanted to put Tical in his place, but there was something about Tical's eyes that made Red think twice about jumping stupid. Red couldn't understand how a guy so young acted like he was the man in charge. Tical wasn't big at that time, but all that would change in the future. He was going to eventually switch the game and deal heroin and become a legend on Baltimore streets and become the Dopeman.

Millie nodded off in the Porta Potty as drool slid down her lip. She quickly yanked back her head as she felt her chin touch her chest. She quickly opened her eyes and looked around the stall, trying to remember where she was. The horrendous smell of urine almost made her gag as she positioned herself upright with the needle still stuck in her arm. She slowly slid the needle from her skin and placed it in her purse. She opened the door and slowly stepped out. She smiled as the air hit her face. It felt good to her and the air tickled her skin and the heroin put her in a place where only junkies could fathom. Millie had no idea at how long she had nodded in the Porta Potty. She hoped she hadn't been in the stall while her stepfather rolled up on her post because she didn't want to hear his mouth when she got home. She walked around the building, preparing to get back on her post so that she could make more money. At that point she had forgotten that she had stolen nearly $500 from her last John. She walked aimlessly to the trucking parking lot as she scanned the lot for potential customers. Her legs wobbled as she caught a nod while walking, almost falling. She almost got hit by a red Lexus that was exiting the lot and she heard the loud horn from the car blowing at her. She stuck up her middle finger and continued to walk as she began to head toward the area where the truckers usually parked. Millie held her head down as she walked uncoordinatedly. She heard a voice yell from a few yards away, so she lifted her head.

"You dirty bitch," a white man screamed as he held a shotgun in his hand. Millie quickly focused on the man's face and noticed that it was the John that she had lifted the cash from.

"Aw fuck!" Millie yelled as she saw the man raise his gun and point it at her. She quickly made a dash for the row of cars a few feet away from her while ducking down. She quickly disappeared in between the cars.

Aw shit, Aw shit, *Millie thought as she ducked down, trying not to be seen by him. She crouched down and maneuvered through the rows of cars trying to shake the ranting man.*

"Where you at, li'l black bitch?" he yelled as he looked around crazily as he went in and out of rows trying to locate her.

Millie quickly dipped by a small truck and heard the man's voice getting closer and closer. Thinking fast, she hopped into the bed of the truck and lay on her back. She positioned herself tightly in between the two big haystacks that sat in the back. She lay flat on her back and stared into the sky, hoping that the man would not find her. After a couple of minutes of lying there, she began to nod because of the potent drug, and fell into a deep nod. She didn't even feel someone get in the car and pull off.

Tical rode down the highway, glancing at the bag that contained the coke in it, and smiled, knowing that he would return home and make money. He wished that he had put the coke into the haystacks like he planned, but when he came out he saw a crazy-ass white man yelling with a gun and he knew that his best bet was to get out of the area before the cops came.

"Mufucka crazy," Tical said to himself as he thought about how crazed the man looked. Tical drove about thirty miles down the highway, heading back to Baltimore, and saw a sign that showed that a rest stop was ahead about three miles. He decided to put the coke in the stash spot at the next stop. Tical pulled his car off at the next exit and spotted a small gas station just off the ramp. Tical drove the truck up to the station and got out and quickly tossed the bag in the back bed. He then headed into the store so he could pay for some gas before he hid the coke into the haystacks.

Millie felt a bag hit her face as she quickly jumped up, not remembering where she was at; heroin had that effect on its users at times. She saw the haystacks surrounding her and she remembered that she had been hiding from the irate John and her heart began to pump quickly. She looked around and saw the unfamiliar setting. "Where the fuck am I?" she said as she began to take the straws of hay out of her hair. She looked at the book bag that was thrown on her and wondered who had tossed it. She looked at the truck and realized that she had nodded while hiding in the back of it. "Fuck!" she said as she wondered how far she was from the truck stop that she posted at. Am I even still in New York? She stepped out of the truck with the bag in her hand. She heard a gun click and she quickly turned around.

"Li'l ma, I don't know who you are, but you barked up the wrong tree," a calm, raspy voice said as he firmly held his gun, while pointing it at her chest. "Red sent you, huh?" he said as he yanked the bag from Millie. He lowered his gun and quickly grabbed Millie by the arm, while checking her for a gun with his other hand. He saw her rise from the back of his truck while he was paying for gas and the first thing that came to his mind was that Red had sent her to rob him for the same product he had just sold to him; an old stick-up kid trick.

"You got five seconds to tell me who sent you or I'ma send one of these slugs through your stomach. Try me!" Tical said, meaning every single word he stated. He noticed how young the girl was and slightly loosened his grip on her. Millie was terrified and it showed through her youthful eyes. She couldn't even get the words out; she just froze in fear.

"I'm sorry, sir. I just hid in the back of your truck because this crazy mufucka was after me. I swear to God!" Millie said as she began to tear up thinking that she was about to die. Tical began to think about the man that he saw screaming in the parking lot and wondered if she was telling the truth.

"What he look like?" he asked, still having a cold tone in his voice.

"He was a white trucker-looking mufucka," Millie said while keeping her eyes on Tical's gun with her hands still in the air. Tical realized that it was possible that she was telling the truth, but he still remained cautious. He stared at her

intently for a few seconds and then decided to ease up. He put his gun back into his waist as he looked around to make sure no one was watching. "Get in the car," he ordered as he pointed to the truck. Millie turned, shaking like crazy, and headed toward the vehicle. She thought about making a dash for it, but she didn't know if he would shoot her in the back. What the fuck have I gotten myself in to? This farmer-looking mufucka about to take me somewhere and rape and kill me, *she thought as she slowly made her way to the passenger side.*

"And put yo' hands down," Tical said as he took one last look around the gas station. He put the coke back in the hidden compartments that were in the haystacks while keeping an eye on Millie through the back window. Once he finished, he got into the car and observed the young girl. He saw her discomfort and he saw that she didn't pose any harm to him. He saw tears forming in her eyes and her jitteriness displayed her terror. Tical sat in the car and remained silent as he wondered if her story was legit. He put his gun on his side for easy access and shook his head, regretting what he was about to say.

"Look, I'm not going to hurt you, so relax. I will take you back to the truck stop, okay?" he said in a nicer tone, trying not to scare the girl any more than he already had. Millie nodded her head in relief, but still remained cautious of him. She didn't know his real intentions. He started up the truck and prepared to go thirty-three miles back and return to the spot, so he could drop her back off at her post. They rode in silence as Tical kept his eyes on the road. Millie was the first to speak.

"So where are you from? I can tell that you are not from around here," Millie said as she began to feel a tad bit more comfortable. Tical didn't even look at her and continued to drive. He had a bad feeling about the girl and couldn't help but feel that he was getting set up, but the good in him didn't let him leave her so far away from where she supposedly was from.

"Chill out with the small talk, ma. I ain't got any convo for you," Tical said as he frowned up.

"Dang, I was just trying to be polite," Millie said as she grew an embarrassed look and began to scratch her arms. Her high had fallen and she began to get the itch that most fiends got after they got high. She felt like an army of small ants was marching up and down her veins.

Tical glanced at Millie's arm and saw the needle marks. He looked at Millie's gestures and knew that she was a user. He began to feel bad about being so rude to her and forced himself to talk to her.

"How old are you anyway?" Tical asked. After a few seconds of silence, Millie noticed that Tical was glancing down at her marks. He continued after not getting a response, "Well, you don't look a day over sixteen and you out here bad. That shit ain't for you," he said as he shook his head in disbelief. They getting younger and younger, *he thought as he switched lanes.*

"How do you know what's for me? I'm a grown-ass woman," Millie lied as she snapped her neck back and forth displaying a major attitude.

"Grown-ass woman, huh?" Tical said. Millie fooled a lot of people, but she couldn't fool Tical. He knew that she was a minor. Although she had a developed body, she didn't have the gestures of a person who had been through life yet. That was always a telltale sign and Tical could scope out that instantly. "You can't be any older than sixteen or seventeen, but whatever you say." He looked at the chocolate girl who sat next to him and for some reason was drawn to her. Maybe it was because she resembled his mother with her skin tone and big, deep brown eyes.

Just as Tical was about to say something, the flashing red and blue lights of a police car shined. "Fuck," Tical said as he calmly glanced in his rearview mirror. Tical pulled his truck onto the side of the road and instantly began to grow big butterflies inside of his stomach. He reached into his waist and discreetly slid his gun to the side of his seat, ready to blast his way out of the situation if the officer caught wind of the kilos in the back of the truck. Millie watched as Tical became noticeably shaken up and as he slid the gun under his shirt while clicking it off safety. He had a life sentence hidden in his haystacks and he had already made up his mind that if the cop asked him to step out he was going to go out blasting. Tical watched as the cop got out of his cruiser and approached the truck.

"Good evening, sir," Tical said as he kept his hand on the steering wheel, already knowing the drill.

"License and registration," the cop said as he kept his hand near his gun.

"No problem," Tical said as he slowly reached over Millie's lap and into the glove box. After retrieving his papers he handed them to the officer. The officer took the papers and suspiciously began to look at the haystacks in the back. The cop went to his cruiser and ran Tical's name, finding out that Tical had a felony from a previous gun charge and he instantly got suspicious and wanted to find out more about Tical. He returned to the car looking for any signs that Tical was up to no good.

"Who is this young lady with you?" the cop asked as he stood on Tical's side.

"This is my younger sister . . ."

"Millie!" Millie said, interrupting him.

Is that right?" the officer asked as he glanced over at her. He walked to the back of the truck and began observing what was in the bed of it.

"What's the haystacks for?" the officer said as he began to take a closer look at them. Tical slightly turned his body to look back at the cop, but when he turned his gun slid off his lap and onto the side of the seat. "Damn," Tical said in a low tone as he saw that the gun had slipped. The officer quickly turned around and approached the window.

"What's that, boy?" the officer said as he slowly placed his hand over his gun.

"Nothing, sir," Tical said as he began to get tense.

"Won't you step out of the car?" the officer said while keeping a close eye on him. He heard the clinking of the metal when Tical had dropped the gun and he quickly got suspicious. Tical, knowing that he had to stay calm and hope that the officer didn't see the gun, stepped out of the car slowly. The officer escorted him to the rear of the truck and told him to turn around. Fuck,

Tical thought, as he knew that he was in a bad predicament. He watched helplessly from the backseat of the cop car as the officer made Millie stand at the rear of the car while he searched it. Tical knew that he was going to find either the gun or the drugs. The gun was in clear sight and he knew that he was caught. After three minutes of waiting for the cop to come out of the truck with the gun . . . nothing happened. The cop made Millie get back in the car and walked back to the patrol car where Tical sat.

"I'm just going to let you off with a warning," he said as he opened the door and let Tical out. Tical was relieved as he slowly stepped out of the car and got the handcuffs removed. Tical could tell in the cop's expression that he was disappointed that he didn't find anything and Tical couldn't help but smirk as he returned to his truck. He got back into the car and looked down at the floor, noticing the gun had been removed. At that moment he knew that Millie had hid it from the cop for him. Tical pulled off and took a deep breath, knowing that he had just dodged a bullet.

"Thanks," Tical said as he glanced quickly over at Millie.

"It ain't nothing," Millie answered as she reached into her pantyhose and pulled out the gun and placed it on Tical's lap.

"So what's your name again?" Tical said as he lightened up and became appreciative of her quick thinking.

"Milian, but everyone calls me Millie."

"You are pretty sharp, I see."

"Yeah, I have to be. The streets tend to keep you on your shit," Millie said, and began to scratch her arms again.

"Who got you started?" Tical asked, referring to her heroin habit. He had seen the best of them go down because of the drug.

"Started on what?" Millie asked while still scratching, causing her arms to slightly bleed. Tical momentary looked down at her arm and nodded his head in its direction. He gave her a look that said, "Don't insult my intelligence."

Millie, seeing that Tical was street smart and could tell that she had a habit, couldn't deny it. "My stepfather," she answered.

"Your stepfather? That's fucked up," he said as he shook his head from side to side. Millie studied Tical's gestures and mannerisms and immediately was attracted. Even though he had on farmer clothes, she knew that it wasn't his style. The way he talked and took his time with every syllable had Millie wanting to learn more about the older man.

Her mind was trained to look at every man as a potential John and that is exactly what she did. Millie unbuckled her seatbelt and took the gum out of her mouth that she was chewing. She then leaned over the seat and attempted to put her head in Tical's crotch, wanting to give him oral sex. Tical immediately put his hand on her forehead and gently pushed her away.

"Fall back, ma. It ain't that type of party," Tical said as he frowned up and looked at Millie like she was insane.

"What's wrong? You don't think I'm pretty?" Millie asked as she grew self-conscious about how she looked. When she was in school, she got teased about her dark skin tone. Millie had hatred for herself ever since she was young. Society had wrongly taught her that the lighter you are, the prettier the person was.

"Actually, I think you are beautiful, but I ain't trying to take it there with you. You are way too young for me," Tical said as he sensed her insecurities.

"You really think I'm pretty?" Millie skeptically asked as she ran her fingers through her damaged hair and placed the gum back into her mouth. She wasn't used to a person telling her how beautiful she was when they had no intention of sexing her.

"I wouldn't say it if I didn't mean it," Tical said. He wanted to change the subject, so he began to ask her common questions and they talked all the way until they reached the truck stop. The hour ride only seemed like minutes to Millie; she had fallen in love with Tical's swagger within the thirty miles they had traveled on the highway. When he pulled up to the stop, she saw her stepfather waiting outside of the diner with a small bottle of five o'clock gin in his hand. Millie's heart instantly began to pump. She knew that every time he drank he would beat and sexually abuse her.

"Okay, here's your stop," Tical said as he put his truck in park and hit the unlock button. Tical looked over at Millie and noticed her discomfort. He followed her eyes and noticed that she was staring at the man who stood in front of the diner. "That's your stepfather, huh?" he asked. Millie nodded her head and became teary-eyed as she thought about the night ahead of her. Tical looked at Millie, then back at her stepfather, and he just couldn't release Millie to the wolves after what she had done for him earlier with the cop. "I'll be right back," he said just before he grabbed his gun and put it in his waist, jumped out of the car, and headed toward the man.

The man who Millie called her stepfather leaned against the building while smoking a cigarette. He had been there for the past thirty minutes looking for Millie. He didn't notice Tical walk up until it was too late. Tical grabbed the man by his collar and slammed him up against the wall aggressively.

"Yo', man, what's yo' damn problem?" he said as he looked confused as he got ambushed. Tical looked deep into the man's eyes while still having a tight grip on him, and although Tical was full of rage, his voice remained calm and clear.

"Yo', is that your daughter in that car right there?" he asked as he threw his head in the direction of Millie, who sat in his passenger side. The man squinted, trying to look inside the car to see.

"Oh, I see what you getting to," he said as he grew more relaxed. "She is a hot commodity around here. Tell you what, give me fifty and you can have her all night. Believe me, she's good. I've tested the goods myself," he said proudly as he puffed his cigarette. Tical couldn't control himself as he quickly wrapped his strong hand around the man's neck and squeezed as tight as he could. The thought of Tical's own mother being killed by an abusive boyfriend when he was only sixteen emerged. Millie looked so similar to his mother, he instantly felt connected to her, and all of the hatred seemed to travel into his hand that was suffocating the man. Tical watched as the man struggled for air and dug his nails into Tical's hand, trying to get him to release him. Tical began to talk to the man, speaking his mind. "You are a bitch-ass nigga. You feeding that li'l girl poison and killing her slowly. She's not even old enough to understand what she's doing to her body. I should put a hole through yo' mufuckin' dome. Niggas like you make me sick. You can't get out here and hustle for yours; you leech off of the weak. But you the weak one!" he said as he emphasized every word that came out of his mouth. He reached and grabbed his pistol from his waist. He then put the barrel of the gun in his mouth and his trigger finger began to itch. Tical stared at the man as he looked as if he was about to lose consciousness and realized that he wasn't even worth the bullet. He released his strong grasp and watched as the man fell to his knees and gasped for air. Tical turned around and walked toward his truck, breathing heavily. Millie looked confused as she sat there in fear, not knowing what Tical was going to do to her. She hadn't heard what was said between the men, she just saw Tical grab her stepfather by the neck. The car was silent, except for Tical's heaving breathing, which eventually slowed down. Tical gathered himself and thought about what he was about to say. He knew that he was about to do something out of character, but deep in his heart he had to.

"You are coming with me, okay?" Tical said as he turned to Millie and stared at her with his piercing hazel eyes. Something came over Millie and in a situation where another girl would've been scared, she became comfortable. She slowly nodded her head in agreement as tears formed in her eyes. Not tears of pain, but of joy. For some unknown reason to her, she knew that from that day on, she would be okay.

From that day on, Tical took Millie under his wing and taught her everything he knew. He looked at her as a younger sister and helped her kick her drug habit and made her return to school. He always told her that her living with him would just be temporary, but weeks turned into months, and month into years. They had become family. Tical helped her kick her heroin habit cold turkey and told her that he would kill her before he let her go down that road again and he meant every word. He refused to let Millie inject poison into her body. He told her that she was on the wrong side of the game, and instead of killing herself with the drug, he taught her how to get rich off the drug. After two years of grooming and on her nineteenth birthday, he introduced Millie to the hustle game and she took to it like a duck took to water. Most people said she was the female version of Tical and rightfully so, as he raised her. Tical had promised her that no matter what they would always be family and always stay close. That's why he made sure that every Friday was their day to bond and talk. Even after she moved out, he wanted to keep their Friday ritual going. He never told her, but he wanted to make sure that Millie never messed with drugs again, and that was his slick way of always checking on her and keeping her close. She was his backbone and he was hers.

Millie snapped out of her nod and looked around her home, hoping she would see Tical . . . but then her harsh reality set in. She wiped the slobber from her mouth and tears from her eyes and staggered to the bathroom to clean herself up. She knew that the only way she could see Tical was in her daydreams.

Chapter Fourteen

Hazel was wiping down the table in Insight's cafeteria. Dr. Young had gotten her a job as a food service worker there and she had been clean going on almost six months. She had visited Apple frequently along with Seven and she could tell that her father was happy to have his little girl back. Hazel glanced at the clock and noticed that she had worked five minutes past her shift, and quickly finished wiping off the long tables and snatched off her hair net. She made her way to the back room where the other cafeteria women were and stuck her head in the door.

"See ya, guys," she yelled as she smiled, sticking half of her body inside the room.

"See ya!" one of the elderly women yelled.

"Bye, Hazelnut!" another one said. Hazel was taken aback at the sound of someone calling her by her nickname. It instantly reminded her of Millie. She exited the facility, telling people bye on her way out, but Millie was the only thing on her mind. Hazel missed Millie so much, it hurt her heart. But a rule of recovery was to separate yourself from former friends who could potentially make you relapse.

Hazel made it to her car and sat in front of her steering wheel, contemplating going to see Millie. *I just want to know that she's okay, that's all,* she thought as she gripped her steering wheel tightly. Hazel no longer had the urge to use heroin and her body was fully detoxed, so she decided that she would go to see Millie just for a second, having confidence in herself not to relapse.

"Sorry, Seven," she whispered as if he could hear her. But that was impossible, because he was on the highway on his way to see Hassan that evening. Seven informed her that he would be staying the night up north to prevent driving back late and would be returning in the morning. That gave Hazel a while without him. Seven would always tell GiGi to check in on Hazel, but she never did. Hazel didn't mind that at all. Hazel started up her Benz and pulled off, heading to Millie's projects.

Hazel was standing in front of Millie's door and had been knocking for two minutes straight. Hazel saw Millie's light creeping from the bottom of her door and heard the television running from the outside. Hazel knew how cheap Millie was and also knew that she wouldn't leave the house with her lights on and the television running. "Come on, Millie. I know you're in there," Hazel whispered as she began to grow impatient. Hazel had had enough of waiting and bent down to pick up the doormat, remembering how Millie always left an extra key under it for emergencies. Just as she thought, a silver key was placed underneath it.

"Bingo," she whispered as she scooped up the key and laid the mat back in its place. Hazel quickly opened the door and walked into the house.

"Millie!" she called as she began to walk through the house in search of her friend. "Millie!" she called again. Hazel's heart began to beat as she approached the bathroom door, instantly throwing her back to her childhood when she found her mother dead in the bathroom with a needle stuck in her arm.

"Millie," Hazel whispered as she placed her hand on the bathroom's doorknob, afraid of what she would find on the opposite side of the door. Hazel slowly turned the knob and opened the door. The first thing she saw was Millie's feet. Hazel opened the door wider, finding Millie with a gown on and a needle sticking out of her arm as she lay limply on the toilet.

"Millie!" Hazel screamed as she put both of her hands over her mouth. Hazel froze as one of her worst fears had come true. She had lost the only woman she had left on earth.

Millie quickly opened one of her eyes and wiped the slobber from the side of her mouth. "Bitch, why you yelling so damn loud? You scared the shit out of me," she said while giving Hazel a small grin.

"Millie!" Hazel screamed as she smiled and wiped the tears that had just fallen from her eyes. She rushed over to the toilet, took the needle out of Millie's arm, and hugged her.

"I thought you were dead!" she said as she hugged her as tight as she could. Mille wrapped her arms around Hazel and began stroking her hair slothfully.

"Girl, you know Millie don't die. I'm the toughest bitch alive," she joked while still slurring her words. Hazel laughed, knowing that Millie hadn't changed a bit, and was still conceited and blunt.

"I missed you, girl," Hazel said as she placed her ear right over Millie's heart.

"I missed you too, Hazel . . . nut," Millie answered. "You look good, baby. Seven taking real goo . . . good care of my girl, huh?" Millie asked as she slowly continued to stroke Hazel's hair.

"Yeah, he's treating me very good, Millie," Hazel said as she closed her eyes and cherished the moment. She missed Millie so much and it just felt good to her just to be in her arms. Hazel began to smell the musty body odor reeking off of Millie and instantly knew that Millie was down bad. Hazel never recalled a time when Millie didn't keep herself or hygiene up. Although Millie had a bad habit, she used to never let her appearance slip, but times had changed. Hazel grabbed Millie and stood up. Hazel looked into Millie's eyes and saw that she had a yellow shade within her pupils and had lost quite a few pounds.

"Damn, Millie," Hazel whispered as she just stared for a minute. Hazel quickly took off her jacket and rolled up her sleeves. She then threw Millie's arm around her and tried to help her into the bathtub so she could run cold water on her; a trick that helps a fiend get out of a nod. Millie had done this so many times for Hazel and now it was a role reversal.

"Come on, girl," Hazel said as she slightly lifted her up, helping Millie get to her feet and into the bathtub. Hazel wasn't too strong so she dropped Millie sort of hard into the porcelain tub.

"Bitch, you dun' hit my head against this hard-ass tub," Millie said teasingly while cheesing from ear to ear with her eyes still closed.

Hazel burst into laughter and felt warm inside, knowing that she was with her partner in crime and best friend once again.

"Sorry," Hazel said, half laughing as she put her hands on her hips and stared at Millie lying there so cool with her head propped against her fist. Hazel turned the knob for the cold water and then reached up, pointing the shower directly at Millie's face. Nothing came out. Hazel frowned and then walked over to the sink and turned the knob for the faucet water to run. Again, nothing.

"Millie!" Hazel yelled as she looked over at her girl. Millie had begun nodding again and her chin was buried into her own chest. "Millie," Hazel yelled again, that time waking Millie. Millie opened one eye and looked at Hazel.

"Your water got turned off?" Hazel asked.

"Yeah, they caught me slipping," Millie said, almost sounding drunk. Hazel shook her head and helped Millie get out of the tub. She was about to take her to Seven's place to clean her up, although Seven had told Hazel never to have company at his spot, being that it was the place that he laid his head. However, Hazel felt that she owed Millie at least that much.

Chapter Fifteen

It was just before midnight and Hazel was on the couch eating popcorn, watching the movie *Dead Presidents*. Millie was in the back room, asleep. Hazel had laid her down about an hour before, after bathing her and lending her a pair of her pajamas.

"How long have I been out?" Millie asked as she walked into the living room.

"About an hour," Hazel answered as she looked back.

"Ooh, I love this movie," Millie said as she walked over to the couch and took a seat next to Hazel. Hazel passed Millie the popcorn and comfortably sat Indian style on Seven's sectional couch.

"This is a nice spot," Millie said as she looked around, admiring the well-decorated three-bedroom apartment. "I would think Seven would be staying in a mansion or something with the paper he is getting," Millie stated.

"Seven's not like that. He isn't flashy," Hazel responded. Millie got up and began to look at the certificate that was in a frame that sat on top of the mantle.

"I was there when you got this. I was so proud of you, Hazelnut," Millie said, thinking back to the day she witnessed Haze receive the award.

"You were for real?" Hazel asked, not believing her.

"Hell yeah, I was there. You had on a blue skirt and white blouse, right?" Millie asked as she briefly looked into space and closed her eyes, trying to recall the time.

"Yeah, that's right," Hazel said as she smiled and was honored.

"That program helped me out so much, Millie. I think you should give it a try. I thought I could've never shook that shit, but I did. Life is so much better when you're not searching for that next high."

"You know what?" Millie said as she placed the certificate back on the mantle. She sat next to Hazel and continued, "That might not be a bad idea. I don't want to be hooked on that shit forever. I tell you what . . ." Millie said as she turned toward Hazel sitting Indian style on the sofa. "You have to name your first baby after me and I will go to that Insight place to get clean," she said, extending her hand.

"Whoa, whoa, you got a deal but where this baby shit coming from? I'm not having any kids. I got to get a man first," Hazel said, laughing her ass off and shaking Millie's hand to solidify the deal.

"I know Seven be hitting them cans. I see you getting thicker back there," Millie said, noticing Hazel looking healthier.

"Girl, please. It's not even like that. It's just since I left them drugs alone, I can keep a little weight on me now, that's all."

Hazel and Millie talked for hours and Hazel dropped Millie off at about 4:00 A.M. Millie had promised her that next time they saw each other, she would be clean. Nevertheless, only time could tell.

Chapter Sixteen

It was the weekend of the boat trip and Hazel was excited, being that she had never been on a boat before. Hazel hadn't heard from Millie since she had seen her a week before when they had spent time with each other. Hazel, along with GiGi, Rah, Toya, and Seven rode in the back of the limo on their way up I-75. Everyone was drinking champagne except for Seven; he just sat back and observed and got pleasure out of everyone else having fun. He looked at GiGi and then back at Hazel. He had to admit, although GiGi was supposed to be the next big thing in the modeling world, Hazel was more attractive on that day in his eyes. The all-white sundress that Hazel wore hugged her waist flawlessly as the bottom half bloomed out and since she hadn't been using drugs six months her eyes were brighter and she had a certain glow about her. *Damn, Hazel looks good when she's cleaned up,* Seven thought. The diamond necklace that he bought for her that hung around her neck shined perfectly in the light. Hazel saw Seven looking at her necklace and she winked at him, like she was saying "thank you" without anybody hearing her. Seven grinned and quickly looked away so GiGi wouldn't catch on. GiGi noticed the necklace too and she was obviously being fake when she gently picked it off her chest and asked, "This is pretty, Hazel. Who got this for you?" GiGi was waiting for her to say Seven's name so she could wild out on him right then and there.

"My daddy," she whispered proudly as she grinned and looked into Seven's eyes. It made Seven smile also, because he knew that she was referring to him rather than Apple. At that exact moment something happened . . . magic. He knew that Hazel was a little more than a friend. GiGi followed Hazel's eyes and looked over at Seven, but he had already looked away just in time for her not to notice.

"Oh, your daddy, huh?" she stated skeptically as she rolled her eyes, sat back, and crossed her arms.

"We're here," Rah said, easing up the tension in the air as the limo exited off the highway and pulled onto the loading deck that was right off the exit. A group of beautiful women wearing skimpy swimsuits and designer shades stood on the deck, waiting to board the yacht along with some of Hassan's Haitian goons. Everyone's attention in the limo turned to the beautiful, luxurious yacht that sat on the water.

"Damn, that's so pretty," Hazel said as she looked on in awe.

"My nigga Hassan does it big," Seven said, assuring them that they were dealing with a millionaire. They all stepped out of the limo wearing their finest threads. Seven had on white linen shorts, no drawers on of course, with a collared, all-white Gucci shirt. His Caesar haircut was lined perfectly, giving him a neat, schoolboy look. To top it off, his cocaine-white Gucci shoes matched perfectly with his attire. A platinum chain hung down to his mid-section as it sparkled against the bright sun. Needless to say . . . he was fly. It was not intentional, but Hazel's sundress matched Seven's hook up exactly and her hair was neatly pulled back, letting her smooth baby hair rest along the edges. The Dolce & Gabbana shades that she picked up while shopping with Seven had white trim and made her feel like a diva. Seven grabbed her hand to help her out of the car and he did the same for GiGi. GiGi was fuming inside, feeling something going on between Seven and Hazel. She smacked her lips loudly as she stepped out, letting Seven know she didn't appreciate him helping Hazel out of the car before her.

"Don't start any shit, G. We came here to have a good time," Seven whispered kindly as he threw his arm around her waist and pecked her on the forehead with a soft kiss. Rah and his lady friend got out of the car and headed toward the loading deck. Hassan was on the yacht looking down at everyone while shirtless. His hair was clipped up and had body and bounce like a model straight out of a shampoo commercial. He ran his fingers through his hair and smiled when he saw Seven and company approaching. Hassan had a bottle of Ace of Spade in his hand and he chugged away as if it weren't a $900 bottle of champagne. Natasha, his head Russian madam, was rubbing sunscreen on his back as he stood there. Natasha's body was immaculate to say the least. She was slim, tall, and had jet-white blond hair; it looked as if it were pure snow. Her Burberry thong bikini left nothing to the imagination and her perky titties hung freely because she didn't wear a top, hating tan lines. Her dark pink nipples stuck straight out like missiles and were at least an inch long. Her six-inch stilettos added to her already tall figure.

"Seven, my friend!" he yelled as he spread his arms out. Seven threw his arms up and returned the smile. "Come on up!" Hassan yelled as he gulped down another swallow of the champagne. The group of people who were talking and standing around parted, making a lane so Seven and his entourage could enter.

Hazel looked up at the big boat and couldn't believe her eyes. She never experienced anything so luxurious in her whole life. In the short time that she had been around Seven, he had exposed her to new cities, new experiences, and a new outlook on life. She climbed the stairs that led to the boat. The sounds of Prince's "Diamonds and Pearls" were playing on the boat as they reached the hardwood, glossy deck. Hassan approached them with smiles while Natasha had a hand full of drinks, handing each of them one.

"Glad you could make it," Hassan said as he walked up and embraced Seven. "And what do we have here?" he said as he looked at the ladies. Seven turned to them and answered.

"This is GiGi, Hazel, Toya, and of course you know Rah," Seven said as he went down the line introducing everyone. Hassan greeted each lady with a smooth kiss on the hand and when he got to Hazel, he was instantly attracted.

"You look familiar," Hassan mentioned as he never let go of Hazel's hand. Hazel blushed, knowing that Hassan was slightly flirting with her. Hassan didn't know, but he was looking into the eyes of one of his old client's daughter.

"That's because she's Apple's daughter," Seven said, interrupting the awkward moment of silence.

"Oh, I see it now. You have the same mark on your face as your father," Hassan said while touching the small apple birthmark under her eye. "Your father was a very good friend of mine. He used to always talk about you when he came to visit me. Shall we?' Hassan said as he stuck out his arm, hoping that Hazel would clutch on; she did. Everyone followed Hassan onto the top deck where more half-naked women were dancing to the music. The other goons boarded the ship and the party began. It was a day that was set to be beautiful as they were going to travel up and down the coast partying. Nevertheless, when something is supposed to be nice . . . it never stays that way.

Millie slowly bobbed up and down on Mouse's shaft as he sat back, naked, while smoking a weed-filled blunt, blowing smoke circles as *SportsCenter* played on the screen. He looked at Millie's slim, chocolate body and almost forgot that she was a dopefiend. Her pretty face, full lips, and abnormally fat vagina had him wondering why she let a potentially beautiful life go to waste at the hands of an addiction. He could see her being wifey material to a hustler of his status, but her addiction put her at the bottom of the totem pole as far as women went in his eyes. There was something about Millie's confidence and her bluntness that attracted Mouse. Millie always seemed to be in charge no matter what the situation. Mouse loved that about her. *Too bad she on that shit,* he thought as he began to pump, cramming his hard pole down her throat. Millie didn't gag once.

"Damn, ma," he crooned as she began to play with his sack while giving him a performance that would put Karrine Stephens to shame. He couldn't take it anymore; he put down his blunt and his toes began to curl. He plunged into her mouth, releasing a walnut-sized glob of his fluids into the back of her throat.

"Uhmm," Millie moaned while she swallowed everything he had to offer. Millie proceeded to suck him bone-dry while she never stopped playing with his sack. She was trying to give him everything he deserved for the two packs of dope and the hundred-dollar bill he had given her. Although Mouse had caught an orgasm, he was still rock hard and ready for more. He had snorted a couple of lines of cocaine just before they started, so it gave him the ability to stay erect longer. Mouse grabbed the condom on the nightstand and quickly slid it on his shaft, letting Millie know he wasn't done yet. Veins were poking out of his tool and his tip was blush red and he stroked himself after putting the protection on correctly. Millie smiled, knowing that she was about to get served right. She loved dealing with Mouse because he always came correct.

Millie licked the tips of her fingers and slowly began to play with her already drenched love box, slipping two fingers inside herself and letting her thumb tease her clitoris simultaneously. She straddled Mouse and her juices began to drip on his inner thigh as he began to play with her small breasts. Millie positioned herself as she grabbed Mouse's pole and directed it into her love box, causing a big slurping noise to sound throughout the room.

"Ooh," she crooned as she slowly began to ride him. She reached behind and played with his sack while moving her body like a snake. Mouse's eyes were fixated on her pink insides and erect clitoris. He spread her lips so he could get a better view.

Millie slowly rode him, digging deep and moaning in pleasure. Millie always gave her best when dealing with Mouse because she knew that the better the sex, the more dope she could squeeze out of him. Millie honestly didn't know if the thought of shooting the dope in her veins got her wet or the actual sex itself. She began to speed up, knowing that the quicker he busted, the quicker she could get into her "dopefiend lean."

"Damn, nigga. That feels so good," she whispered as she began to speed up, feeling an explosive orgasm coming. Millie was a squirter, so all of her juices leaked onto Mouse as they shot from her vagina like a small faucet. That sight alone made Mouse get hornier as he began to reach his own climax. Mouse's body jerked and Millie quickly jumped off of him, knowing that she had done her job. Mouse's body shook briefly and his toes cracked as he tried to sit up but ended up landing flat on his back in the middle of the queen-sized bed at the Holiday Inn. Mouse was addicted to Millie's sexual performances that she had been giving him frequently. Her sex was the best he had ever had and he never expected that coming from an addict. His mind instantly began to think about her girl, Hazel. He wondered if she was as good as Millie.

"What was li'l mama name that you was with awhile back? With the fat ass. She gets down?"

Mouse asked, referring to tricking for money or dope.

"You talking about Hazel? No, that's my baby! She's off-limits, Mouse. She green to the game anyway. She doesn't even get high anymore. She is off-limits, you hear me?" Millie said with a stern tone, being overprotective of Hazel as she grabbed a towel and dried off her inner thighs. She then reached for her pack of Newports and pulled one out, placing it between her middle and index fingers, lighting it, and taking a deep pull.

"Okay, okay," Mouse half laughed as he propped up on his elbows, knowing that he hit a nerve by asking Millie that. "I was just saying," he said as he watched Millie get up and head to the bathroom. Her petite ass made him think about round two and the gap in between her legs gave him a nice view of her hanging vagina as she disappeared into the bathroom.

"Anyway, she so far up that nigga Seven's ass . . . she ain't trying to fuck nothing but him," Millie yelled while she cleaned up. Mouse couldn't believe his ears. He sat up at the sound of Seven's name and a light bulb popped up in his head.

"Seven?" he asked, playing dumb and trying to get more information out of her.

"Yeah, this nigga from the north side. She's living with him now. He's helping her out and she got her shit together and quit doing drugs."

"Word? That's his girl a' something?" he asked, growing more interested by the second.

"Naw, she just a friend, I guess. The nigga trying to play Superman and keep her clean," Millie said as she got into the shower.

Mouse had a bitter taste in his mouth about Seven because of him shorting the brick of *Lady Luck* awhile back. Seven had also cut him off and his drug operation had suffered because of it. The dope connect that he had currently was more expensive and a lower grade of quality. He promised himself that when he could get Seven back, he would. The golden door of opportunity presented itself to him and he was about to walk through it with pistols.

"She lives with him, huh? Do you know where the spot is?" Mouse said as he sat up and smiled. He was willing to give Millie as much dope as she wanted for the valuable information. He was about to show Seven that shorting him was the worst move he could ever make.

Bottles of champagne flowed into flute glasses and eventually into the stomachs of everyone on the yacht, except Seven's; he was just enjoying the scenery. He sat back and observed the spacious dance floor while slowing bobbing his head to latest R and B hit. He watched as Hazel danced with Hassan, flowing angelically as Hassan guided her movements. Her dress blossomed at the bottom as Hassan spun her around while they laughed together. GiGi danced with one of Hassan's goons on the other side of the floor since Seven had turned her down earlier. Seven never danced, he would always just sit back and watch like only a gangster would. He sipped on a glass of water and raised his glass to Rah who was slow grinding on his date. Seven focused back on Hassan and Hazel and noticed how he held Hazel close and he began to thrust his hips to her like a Latin dancer. Seven got heated, but didn't let it show. GiGi periodically would glance over at Seven, hoping that he would get jealous and cut in, but he never did. His attention was on Hazel and the look on Hazel's face made him become more attracted to her by the second. She was smiling and she seemed like she was having a great time. That alone made Seven grow a small smirk. The current song ended and the sounds of Jackson 5's "I'll Be There" sounded through the speakers. The melodic tune was familiar to everyone in attendance and gasps and claps erupted, everyone remembering the late King of Pop.

"This is my song," Hazel yelled as she threw both of her hands in the air and snapped them while swaying back and forth, temporarily closing her eyes, immersing herself into the classic song. She looked over at Seven and saw him smirking and it was as if she read his mind. Whatever he was feeling at that exact moment, she felt the same thing. She told Hassan that she would finish dancing with him later and turned in the direction of Seven. Hassan put his hands on his chest in disappointment and smiled.

"You're leaving me, sweetheart? You're breaking my heart," he said jokingly as he grabbed a glass of champagne from the bypassing waitress. "I have to dock the boat anyway. Our stop is coming up," Hassan said, referring to the small dock stop a few miles away.

Hazel made her way over to Seven and never once did they break eye contact, both of them smiling while gazing into each other's eyes. Hazel slowly approached Seven and grabbed both of his hands, pulling him up to his feet

"Uh-uh, ma. You know better," Seven said while smiling. "I don't dance."

"Please, Seven. This is my song," Hazel begged as she began to pout her lips and gave him her puppy dog eyes. Seven smiled and shook his head as they both began to chuckle. He reluctantly let her lead him to the dance floor. Rah looked at Hazel leading Seven onto the dance floor and couldn't believe that she had gotten him to slow dance.

"Aw shit! Seven 'bout to cut a rug!" Rah acknowledged as he laughed and continued to dance with his date.

"Chill out," Seven mumbled while shaking his head and grinning as Hazel led him to the middle of the floor. Hazel wrapped her hands around Seven's neck and looked up at him. Seven didn't do too much dancing; he just swayed back and forth while looking back down at her.

"Thank you for bringing me here. I never seen anything like this," Hazel admitted.

"It's beautiful, right?" Seven smoothly added with his signature low, even baritone.

"Yeah, it is. I have something to tell you, Seven."

"What's that, Miss Hazel Brown?" Seven said as he looked at Hazel and leaned in close to her, grinning. He wanted to kiss her, but he immediately thought about GiGi who was only a few yards away from them dancing, not even paying attention to their intimate encounter. Seven stepped back away from Hazel and looked over at GiGi who was now looking at them. She placed her hands on her hips and strutted toward them.

"Oh shit. Here she goes," Rah said as he smiled and joked with Seven. Rah already knew how GiGi could act sometimes. He had witnessed her wild out on Seven plenty of times and he knew something was about to pop off, and he had a front row seat to the show GiGi was about to put on.

"Damn," Seven whispered under his breath and he dropped his head and shook it from side to side, knowing that GiGi was about to act a straight fool.

"What the fuck is all this?" GiGi asked as she stepped in between them, facing Seven, with her hip cocked to the side while resting her right hand on it.

"Chill. It ain't even like that, G," Seven said, trying to calm her down. He put both of his hands in front of himself trying to get GiGi to fall back.

"Fuck that! You all in this bitch face cheesing and shit!" she said as she snapped her neck trying to emphasize her point.

"Who you calling a bitch?" Hazel said as she grabbed GiGi by her shoulder, spinning her around. "I ain't the one! I got your bitch all right," Hazel retorted as she quickly took off her earrings in one swift motion. Before GiGi could respond, Seven pulled her back and told Hazel calmly to leave. Everyone began to look at the brewing fiasco and was waiting for something to happen. It seemed like everyone had stopped dancing and all eyes were on them at that point.

"Let me handle this, Hazel," Seven exclaimed.

"You better control your bitch then. I'm five seconds off that ass, please believe me!" Hazel said, ready to give GiGi what she had been asking for . . . an ass whooping. GiGi mugged Hazel until Hazel eventually smacked her lips and followed Seven's request, not wanting to ruin the night.

"Look, G. You got to stop tripping. I told you before: me and her are not like that. She is like my family."

"Fuck that family shit. She want to fuck you, and the way you acting, you want to fuck her too," GiGi said, getting more upset as she thought about Seven dancing with Hazel and not her, after she practically begged him for thirty minutes straight only to get turned down.

"Fuck that supposed to mean?" Seven asked, not making any facial expression. He was calm, cool, and collected, which only made GiGi more irate.

"Fuck you and that bitch. I'ma end up quitting yo' ass over that dopehead ho. Watch!"

That was all Seven needed to hear. He was about tired of GiGi anyway. The boat was approaching the dock and he saw Hassan at the top steering the yacht, shirtless, with a bottle in his hand, and got a great idea.

"You know what, you right. I'm tripping, G," Seven said. GiGi smiled, thinking that she had Seven wrapped around her finger.

"Yo', let's go over here and talk," Seven suggested as he grabbed GiGi's hand and guided her over to the ledge. As GiGi walked over, thinking that Seven was about to baby her, he did the complete opposite. He scooped her up and tossed her out of the boat, causing everyone to burst out into laughter. They were only a few feet away from the dock so he knew that the water eventually would get shallow and she wouldn't drown. He knew GiGi was a great swimmer, so he didn't feel bad at all for tossing her overboard. Just for good measure he grabbed a life jacket and tossed it overboard right along with her ass.

"Aghhh!" she yelled as she fell butt first into the water. She doggy paddled and couldn't believe what had just happened. Seven had done it so fast, she never saw it coming.

"Have a nice life, ma!" Seven said while laughing, not being able to contain himself. It was one of the funniest things he had ever seen.

"I hate you!" GiGi yelled after she spit water from her mouth and floated. She was more embarrassed than anything. Everyone rushed over to the ledge, including Hazel, and laughed at her as she doggy paddled toward the dock.

"Catch a cab home!" Seven yelled as he went into his pocket and pulled out a wad of cash and let it rain into the water. He looked back at Hassan who was watching from the top, laughing his ass off, almost rolling on the floor. "Yo', let's stop at the next dock!" Seven yelled up, wanting to leave GiGi there alone with the tourists and dockworkers.

"No problem, my friend," Hassan said as he began to turn the boat. GiGi finally got to the dock and the dockworkers helped her get on the boardwalk. She immediately threw up her middle finger and was steaming mad. Seven then grabbed Hazel and gave her a short, wet kiss, only aggravating GiGi that much more as she watched. The yacht drifted off, leaving her feeling dumb and alone. Everyone on the boat held up their drinks, agitating GiGi even more.

A chill went up Hazel's body as Seven's lips touched hers. He gave her a feeling that no man had ever given her. She knew at that moment she wanted no one else but him. He looked into her eyes and gently rubbed her lower cheek with the back of his hand. Without saying anything, he said so much . . . Seven was falling for her.

Chapter Seventeen

It was just approaching midnight and Hassan's yacht was on cruise as they headed back home. Hassan and Seven were inside of the captain's quarters. The room's floor was red velvet and was spacious and luxurious. Hassan stood in the big front window that overlooked the main deck. He had both hands behind his back as he watched his guests dance the night away.

Natasha, Hassan's leading lady, stood behind the bar listening in on their conversation as she always did.

"Seven, it is a beautiful night. Don't you agree?" he asked as he turned around, smiling.

"Yeah, it's cool," Seven answered as he watched Natasha come from behind the bar and hand Hassan a small glass of cognac. Hassan gently kissed Natasha on the cheek and whispered something in her ear. Natasha quickly nodded her head and exited the room. Seven automatically knew that Hassan had just requested privacy for Seven and himself. Hassan watched Natasha leave and then focused his attention on Seven.

"You sure you don't want a drink?" Hassan asked as he raised his glass.

"You know better," Seven said as he smirked.

Hassan smiled as he took a sip and pointed at Seven. " I had to try," he said as he began to pace the room slowly.

"This is a nice boat. I might get me one of these," Seven said as he took another look around and began to rub the velvet couch he sat on.

"You have a long way to get one of these. Many more bricks to flip, my friend."

Seven didn't like Hassan's answer. He took it as him trying to say that he couldn't get on Hassan's level, but Seven chalked it up to Hassan's arrogance rather than disrespect. *I'ma get one, homeboy, trust,* Seven thought as he nodded his head up and down.

"We always talk bricks. Let's talk about other goods . . . you know . . . more precious merchandise," Hassan suggested while continuing to pace the floor.

"What might that be? More precious merchandise?" Seven asked, not understanding what exactly Hassan was getting at.

"Let's cut to the chase, my friend. That lady down there . . . Hazel. She is a very attractive woman," Hassan said as he stopped in his tracks and looked Seven in the eyes. "I want to feel that pussy and I will pay top dollar for her," he said bluntly, meaning every single word.

"What?" Seven asked, not believing what Hassan was getting at.

"You heard me. I said . . . I want to feel that pussy. So, what's it going to cost me?" he asked just before he downed the last of his cognac.

"First of all, that's not my woman and I'm not her pimp. Second, she isn't for sale." Seven sat up, totally feeling disrespected. But then he had to realize that Hazel wasn't his girl and he had to stick to the script. "She's a big girl, so you should approach her yourself and not through me. I have nothing to do with that," Seven added.

"Okay, I think I will," Hassan said, feeling the tension in the room. He smiled, trying to lighten the mood. "We are close to shore. So, if you would excuse me, I have to captain the ship," he said as he turned his back to Seven and looked out the window that overlooked the lower deck, once again placing his hands behind his back. Seven quickly scoffed and shook his head as he got up and left Hassan in the room alone.

When Seven reached the bottom deck, he saw Hazel sitting at a table laughing and talking to Rah and his date. The yacht's loud horn sounded, signaling that they were about to approach the dock. Seven felt his temperature rising and for what Hassan just asked him, he wanted to punch him square in the face. Seven, at that moment, knew that he had caught feelings for Hazel. The yacht docked and everyone exited the boat. Seven saw Hassan pull Hazel to the side and then pass her his card. Hazel kind of frowned, but accepted the card and stuck it in her purse. Seven made a mental note to keep Hazel away from Hassan from that point on.

Chapter Eighteen

Seven gently kissed Hazel in the back of the limo and her supple breasts were exposed as Seven caressed them slowly. Hazel's dark, hardened nipples were pointed straight forward as Seven played with them by massaging them in between his fingers strategically. It didn't take them any time to jump all over each other after the limo driver dropped Rah and his date off. As soon as Rah closed the limo's door they pounced on each other, both feeling the sexual tension between one another. It was long overdue.

"That feels so good," Hazel moaned as she closed her eyes and threw her head back, giving Seven open access to her neck. Seven slid his tongue down and began to suck on her neck as his hand wandered down to her love box. As soon as Seven's finger reached her treasure, he felt the soaking wet panties and it surprised him; she was drenched. He quickly pulled her panties to the side and quickly located her throbbing ball and rubbed it in tiny, swift, circular motions as he continued to tongue kiss her neck as softly as he could. Hazel began to squirm and moan faintly as she parted her legs slightly for Seven.

"Please, put it in," Hazel whispered as she felt the tingling sensation of an early orgasm approaching.

"Hold on, ma. I'ma do this right," Seven whispered as he briefly stopped kissing her and looked into her eyes. He wanted to make love to her in a bed and not in a backseat of a vehicle. Seven was about to grow her up. Seven and Hazel kissed each other gently for the rest of the ten-minute ride home and it was the best thing Hazel had ever experienced.

When finally reaching Seven's home they were both hot and ready to make love. They began to tear each other's clothes off while going up the stairs while kissing. Hazel grabbed Seven's thick rod through his denims and was impressed by his thickness and couldn't wait to feel it inside of her. Mrs. Dixon peeked her head out of her door, attempting to tell Seven something, but he was too busy snatching off Hazel's clothes to mind her.

"Hold on, girl. I gotta get my keys out," Seven said while laughing as Hazel's eyes were focusing on unbuckling his pants.

"Hurry up, negro," Hazel answered playfully and she kissed on his chest and put her back against his apartment's door.

"Oh. Hey, Mrs. Dixon," Seven said as he noticed her looking at him, like she wanted to tell him something. Seven slid his key into the door and they stumbled into his home, both of them half naked, ready to get it on.

The lights popped on, but it surprised Seven because he wasn't the one to flick the switch. The first thing he saw was Mouse sitting on the arm of his sofa with a shotgun. His goon stood in the middle of the room with a snub nose handgun pointed directly at Seven's head. Seven wanted to reach for his gun but he had already stepped out of his jeans and the gun was on his belt's holster and far out of reach. Hazel was still into the moment, not knowing that they were getting ambushed. She noticed Seven stop touching her and she looked at his distraught facial expression.

"What's wrong?" she questioned as she breathed heavily while one of her breasts was exposed, hanging out of her bra. Seven remained silent as he stared at Mouse, clenching his jaws tightly in anger. Hazel followed Seven's eyes and turned around to see what had him so tight.

"Aggh," Hazel screamed as she jumped back, noticing a gun pointed directly at her by Mouse.

"Shut that bitch up," Mouse demanded as he shot a look at his goon. The goon immediately used his free hand to grab Hazel by the throat, shutting her up instantly. The goon then pointed the gun to Hazel's head and bit his bottom lip in anticipation of her gut being splattered everywhere.

"Wait!" Seven said as he threw both of his hands up. "Let her go. She ain't got nothing to do with this."

"I'm the one with the gun. So . . . I guess that makes me in charge, right?" Mouse asked sarcastically as he stood up and pressed his shotgun's barrel to the chest of Seven. "Take her in the back and tie her up," Mouse directed his goon while never taking his eyes off of Seven.

"You sure you want to do this, Mouse?" Seven said as veins began to form in his temples because he was clenching his jaws so tightly. Mouse had heard enough and struck Seven in the face with the butt of his gun, causing his eye to instantly swell up and bleed. Seven dropped to the floor and Hazel quickly knelt to her knee and tried to pick him up.

"Stop! Please stop!" she begged desperately as she tried to help Seven up. Mouse swiftly grabbed Hazel by the hair and snatched her up. He then tossed her to his goon and threw his head in the direction of the back, signaling him to take her in the back and tie her up.

Mouse picked up Seven's gun and slid it in his back pocket, continuing to hold Seven at gunpoint at point blank range.

"Come up off those bricks, my nigga. You can play if you want to. If I don't see cash or them bricks in a couple seconds, I'ma have my nigga bust that pussy open and then kill yo' bitch back there. Then I'ma kill you after you watch. So what's it going to be? It's on you," Mouse said with the look of the devil in his eyes. He was ready to act on all of his threats if Seven didn't play ball.

"I don't have anything here accept for a few thousand. The money and bricks are at another spot," Seven said, willing to give up his money in trade for Hazel's safety. If Hazel wasn't involved he would have spit in Mouse's face, not giving him the satisfaction of robbing him; he would have died for this no doubt. But more was at stake . . . Hazel.

"Don't play with me, nigga!" Mouse yelled, not wanting to hear that the goods were elsewhere. He struck him in the eye with the butt of his shotgun, causing blood to leak from it.

"Fuck!" Seven yelled as he grabbed his eye that felt like it was hanging out of the socket.

Seven came to the realization that Mouse wasn't
going to let Hazel or him live after the robbery so
he was about to go all out. Seven quickly grabbed
the barrel of the shotgun, trying to wrestle it
away from Mouse. The gun went off, sending
buck shots into Seven's front door, making it
resemble Swiss cheese. Seven overpowered
Mouse and got on top of him, but Mouse still
had a firm grip of the gun, not letting it go.
Blood was in Seven's eyes so he could barely see
straight. Mouse's goon came from the back of
the apartment to see what had happened. When
he saw Mouse and Seven tussling on the ground,
he immediately tried to aim his gun for Seven's
head, but couldn't get a good shot on him.

Hazel was in the back tied up and had to listen
helplessly to the terrifying sounds of what was
happening in the front room. Her hands and feet
were duct taped and a sock was stuffed in her
mouth as tears streamed down her face and she
whimpered, hoping that she was just in a bad
nightmare.

Back in the living room, Seven and Mouse still
wrestled for position and the goon waved his
gun around frantically, not knowing if he should
shoot. Seven gained possession of the shotgun
and quickly shot a round at the goon, at the
same time the goon was shooting Seven catching

him in the arm. However, Seven's shot caught the goon square in the chest, blowing him back about three feet and slamming him into the wall.

Seven dropped the shotgun because of the wound to his arm, giving Mouse a chance to grab the pistol in his back pocket and shoot Seven. The bullet caught Seven on the side of his head, dropping him instantly. Mouse quickly stood up and saw that Seven was dead. He looked over at his goon and saw him struggling for air as blood leaked out of his body. Mouse quickly stepped over Seven's body and picked up his goon. "Come on, my nigga. Let's get out of here. You gon' be okay," Mouse said to him as he helped him up and out of the door. Mouse stopped just before he exited and looked back, remembering Hazel was left alive in the back. He was just about to go back there and blow her brains out, but Mrs. Dixon stepped out of the door and Mouse quickly helped his man out of the apartment before she got a good look at him.

Mouse's goon died on the way to the hospital, needless to say. So in the botched robbery Mouse came out with nothing but a dead friend. Also without any bricks of heroin or money. It was all for nothing and Mouse found out quick that karma was real.

Chapter Nineteen

"Hazel," Seven whispered as he slowly crawled into his bedroom with blood leaking from his head and eye. "Hazel," he repeated, so low that she couldn't even hear him. Hazel finally spotted Seven crawling at a snail's pace toward her. The blood that he was covered in horrified her as she watched as he gave his last ounce of energy to get to her. She kicked and squirmed, trying to encourage him to keep coming and that's exactly what he did, giving it his all. Seven finally reached her and unwrapped her, giving her the use of her arms. Just as Hazel got free, Seven collapsed, going unconscious.

"Seven!"

The double doors flung open and Seven lay on a stretcher as the paramedics rushed him into emergency. Hazel ran along with Seven, trying to keep up, and holding his hands tightly, praying that he didn't die.

"Miss, I'm sorry but you can't go in here with him. You will have to wait in the waiting area," a male nurse said as he stopped Hazel as she tried to follow Seven into the operating room. Hazel quickly kissed Seven on his forehead while he had an oxygen mask covering half of his face.

"I'm going to be right here waiting for you when you get out," Hazel said as she lifted up and held his hand tightly, hoping that it wouldn't be the last time she saw him alive.

Hazel went to the waiting room and waited patiently for the doctors to come and tell her Seven's status. *Please God, let Seven be okay. He is a good man and deserves his place on this Earth. Please, God,* she thought as she buried her face in her hands.

Rah came rushing into the hospital, furious. "Where's my man?" he yelled with a look of total rage in his eyes. "Where's Seven?" Rah yelled as he slammed both of his hands on the receptionist's desk and clenched his jaws tightly.

"Sir, you have to calm down," the nurse said as she was noticeably scared of the angry man who looked her dead in the eyes.

"Fuck that! Where is Sev . . . I mean, where is Fredrick Callaway?" Rah said, stating Seven's government name.

"Sir, he is in operation. You will have to wait out there with the others," she said as she scooted away from her desk near the phone, just in case she would have to call security. Rah slammed his fist on the desk and turned around, seeing Hazel sitting there, crying.

"Hazel!" he said as he rushed to her and knelt down to be eye level with her. "What happened?" he asked.

"They were waiting in the house for us when we came and started asking about a stash . . ." Hazel said before Rah put his hand over her mouth so she wouldn't say too much.

"Let's go out here and talk," he whispered and he stood up and headed to the hallway out of earshot of the people waiting in the waiting room.

"Now, tell me what happened again," Rah said as he looked around to see if anyone was paying attention to him.

"That nigga Mouse was waiting in Seven's crib, waiting to rob him. They pulled me into the back and tied me up," Hazel began to cry hysterically but Rah grabbed her by the shoulders and stood her up, making her look him in the face.

"Finish!" he said angrily as his eyes were bloodshot red with anger, sensing something fishy with Hazel.

"That's all! Mouse and his boy was there waiting and then they shot Seven while I was tied up in the back," she said, telling him the best way she could.

"Fuck that! How that nigga know where Seven spot was? You set him up? Huh?" Rah asked as he wrapped his hand around Hazel's neck tightly. Rah quickly let her go, knowing that he let his anger get the best of him.

"No, no. I would never do that. You know that, Rah," Hazel said, feeling heartbroken that Rah would suspect her in doing something so treacherous to their inner circle. Rah had also become like family to Hazel and it hurt her knowing that he doubted her loyalty. Rah instantly calmed down and felt bad for putting his hands on her. He hugged her tightly and hoped for the best for his best friend, Seven. They returned to the waiting room waiting to hear from the doctors.

Four Days Later

Seven lay in the hospital bed just waking up from a short coma. Rah had made sure that after his surgery to remove the bullet from his skull, he was taken to a top floor under an assumed name.

"You're up," a voice said from the corner of the room. It was Rah, who was sitting and waiting for his friend to come to.

"Rah-Rah," Seven called as he held his hand out. Rah got up and walked over to Seven, grabbing his hand firmly. "Where is Hazel?" he said slowly, feeling the dryness in his mouth from the lack of liquids.

"She is at Toya's house. She's cool. She didn't get hurt," Rah assured him. Seven nodded his head, feeling relieved that she wasn't harmed. He tried to move but he was unaware that he had no motor skills on the left side of his body because the bullet hit nerves that blocked his brain's communication with that part of his body.

"The doctor said you wouldn't be able to use you left side for a while. You have to learn how to use it again," Rah said, not holding anything back. Seven closed his eyes and a wave of disappointment overcame him, but he quickly shook it off and began to think about revenge.

"That nigga Mouse tried to kill me," Seven whispered.

"I know. That nigga is dead, you hear me? I got you. I was just waiting for you to wake up and confirm what went down. People in the streets saying that you dead. That nigga Mouse think shit is sweet," Rah said, getting more heated with every word.

"Word?" Seven whispered.

"Yep, he didn't waste any time. He got niggas thinking he took you out, but he got another think coming."

"No doubt."

"So how do you think he found the spot? It's low key and you never let anyone know where it's at," Rah said, not wanting to just come out and say exactly what he was thinking, which was that Hazel had something to do with it.

"I don't know. But I tell you one thing; I'm going to find out," Seven said. He took a deep breath and closed his eyes again. "I'm sleepy. Make sure Hazel is here when I wake up. I have to ask her about a couple of things," Seven said, as he didn't want to believe the obvious.

"I got you. Rest up, fam," Rah said as he bent over and kissed Seven on top of the head and exited the room.

Millie sat in her apartment pacing back and forth while she smoked a Newport cigarette. Pains shot through her stomach as she kept eying the pack of dope that sat on her coffee table. She had been having pains for the past five days and had not touched it since, but her hunger for it grew more and more each day.

"No, Millie! Do it for Hazelnut!" Millie said aloud, talking to herself and trying to coach her way out of temptation's grasp. Millie had used Hazel's achievement as inspiration for her own road to recovery. But it was harder than it seemed. She was aching for a fix and at her wit's end. She had caused Seven's robbery and it was eating at her. She thought Seven was dead and guilt was eating her inside out. For so many years Millie had been using heroin and she was currently on her longest drug-free stretch in years. She was going on five days without shooting up. Millie had a good heart, but at times drugs darkened a person's soul and made them something that they never thought they could be. Millie thought about how she was responsible for getting Hazel on drugs and once Hazel finally found someone to help her get her life together, she got him killed. Millie rarely cried because of how the game had hardened her, but on that day she dropped tears. She quickly wiped them away, stormed toward the table, and grabbed the dope. She then rushed to the bathroom and flushed it down the toilet. Just over a hundred dollars worth was down the pipes and she felt good after doing it. She decided to head to Insight just as she promised Hazel that she would do.

Hazel stood over Seven while he was out and looked down at him, glad that he was alive. Rah sat in the corner of the room waiting for Seven to come to. Hazel sensed something was wrong because Rah was very cold toward her when she arrived with Toya.

"Seven," Hazel said lightly as she rested her hand on top of Seven's. The sight of the bandages wrapped around Seven's head and a bloody spot where he had been shot sent chills up Hazel's back. Seven began to come to and he opened one eye, looking at Hazel.

"Hazel, how you doing, beautiful?" he asked as if he weren't the one lying in a hospital bed.

"I'm okay. I was about to ask you the same thing."

"I'm good. One bullet can't stop me," he said, giving her a small smirk.

Hazel smiled back, not saying anything. Seven tried to prop himself up with his right arm. He wanted to be sitting upright when he asked Hazel a couple of important questions. "I want to ask you something and I want you to be truthful with me, okay?"

"You know I wouldn't lie to you. What is it?" she asked.

"Did anyone approach you about setting me up? Anyone?"

"No, of course not, Seven. You know I would never do anything like that. After all that you have done for me, I would be crazy.

"Okay, okay," Seven said, feeling reassured. But he wanted to ask her another thing to make sure that she had nothing to do with him getting almost killed in his own home. "Have you ever brought anyone to my house and let anyone know where I lived?"

"No, of course . . . Hold up. One night, I let Millie come over and clean up. But it was just for a couple of hours while you were on a run."

"Damn, Hazel," Seven said as he closed his eyes and sunk the back of his head deep into his pillow. "I told you specifically, never bring *anyone* to the spot. I told you," he stated with heavy disappointment in his voice.

"But I—"

"But what?" he yelled as the sound of his heart monitor began to beep faster. "But what?" he asked in a calmer tone. "That's how he caught me slipping. That's exactly how! You betrayed me. You betrayed me," Seven said as he looked away, not even wanting to look at Hazel anymore. "Rah!" he yelled as his jaws were tight and clenched. Rah stood up and walked over to the opposite side of the bed that Hazel stood on.

"What's up, Seven," he answered.

"Give her ten stacks and drop her ass off on a corner. I never want to see her again," he said cold-heartedly.

"Okay," Rah said.

"Wait, Seven. Don't. Please," Hazel said, feeling like a ton of bricks had just fallen on her.

"Get out," Seven whispered.

"Seven, plea—" Hazel began to say before getting cut off.

"Now!" Seven yelled.

"Seven, I love you. You don't have to worry about seeing me again. And I don't need your money," she said just before storming out and slamming the room's door.

"Damn," Seven whispered as he shook his head from side to side, feeling hurt because of what he had just done. He knew that Hazel needed him, but her disloyalty almost cost him his life and he was a hustler who always stuck to the rules. She had to get cut out of his life because maybe the next time he would not be so lucky.

"Want me to go after her?" Rah asked, not knowing what Seven really wanted to do and noticing the regretful look on his face.

"Nah, let her go. I'm done with her. But her girl, Millie. That's how homeboy found out about my spot. I would put a million dollars on it. She was the link. The dopefiend almost got me killed. Handle that for me. Make it painful," Seven said, putting in the order for Millie's death.

"I got you. What about Mouse?" Rah asked, feeling his trigger finger begin to itch.

"You say the streets think I'm dead, right? Let's let that work for us. Let Mouse think it's all good and then I'ma give him something. Something hot, feel me? I will handle that though. Just take care of Millie," Seven said putting everything together in his mind.

Chapter Twenty

Rah's eyes scanned the sidewalks and alleys as he slowly rolled through the projects looking for Millie. He had something to handle with her on behalf of Seven. "Where you at, bitch?" Rah whispered to himself as he slowly turned a corner. Rah saw Li'l Rico standing on the block posted against a light pole, obviously hustling. Rah went to plan B and pulled over his all-black-on-black Hummer. He rolled down the window and stuck his head out of the window. Li'l Rico grew a nervous look on his face as he stood straight up and looked at Rah. He swallowed what seemed like an apple down his throat as Rah mugged him briefly without saying a word. Word on the street was Seven was dead, and Rico didn't know how Rah was going to play it.

"Li'l Man! Come here!" Rah said as he waved him over. Rico looked around and then hesitantly stepped off of the post and toward Rah's car.

"What's up, big homie," Rico said as he slipped his out-of-sight hand toward the gun that was tucked in his waist.

"Yo, you saw that bitch Millie 'round here today?" Rah asked as he checked his rearview mirror.

"Naw, not today. I haven't seen her in a couple of days. What, you wanna trick with her a' something?" Li'l Rico asked without thinking. Rah instantly frowned up and got offended.

"Listen, li'l nigga, I don't have to pay for pussy. And I'm the one asking all the questions, feel me?" Rah said sternly as he looked into the youngster's eyes. Li'l Rico nodded his head and broke eye contact, not wanting any trouble with Rah.

"But check this out. I need a favor."

"Yeah, what up," Li'l Rico said as he thought he was about to earn some stripes and move up on the hustlers' totem pole.

Rah reached into his cup holder and pulled out a pack of dope, *Lady Luck* to be exact. It was wrapped in a small, red rubber band. "I want you to give this to Millie when you see her. Tell her it's some new shit that you want her to check out for you. Understand?" Rah said as he checked his rearview mirror again and dropped it in Li'l Rico's palm.

"Okay, I got you," Rico said as he also took a look around and then dropped it in his pocket after receiving it.

"Make sure you remember. Give her the one with the rubber band around it."

"Red rubber band. Gotcha," Li'l Rico said.

"And this is another rubber band . . . for you, of course," Rah joked as he pulled out a wad of money that was wrapped in a rubber band.

"Cool," Li'l Rico said calmly as he took the money and walked away. Rah pulled off, smiling. It was done. Millie's life was on a countdown. She had a rat poison-laced pack of dope waiting for her. She would feel karma in its deadliest form in due time.

Just as Rico anticipated, not even thirty minutes later he spotted Millie walking to the store. He smiled as he approached her. He had a special delivery for her.

Hazel hurriedly packed her bags, not knowing her next move. She could still smell the stale scent of blood throughout Seven's apartment. The trail of Seven's blood to the room she was in made her get flashbacks to the horrible acts that were committed only days before. She stuffed her clothes in garbage bags and had no idea what her next move was. Seven had just broken her heart. She never meant to be the cause of all the drama, but he never would understand that. For all that Hazel knew, Millie might not have had anything to do with the robbery.

"Damn!" she yelled as she carried the bags out the door. She stuffed them into her trunk and almost forgot her certificate from Insight. She rushed upstairs and grabbed the certificate, stared at it, and knew that if she had gotten herself clean, that she could do anything. With or without Seven.

Hurt and heartbroken, she left and headed to the only place she knew she had left: Millie's home.

Chapter Twenty-one

Hazel pulled into the projects and parked her car near Millie's spot. She took a deep breath and griped as she thought about what she was going to say to Millie when she saw her. She hadn't been dealing with her and now Hazel was running back to her and asking her to take her in. Hazel had saved up about $1,800 from working at Insight, but that was all that she had to her name.

"Here goes nothing," Hazel whispered as she grabbed her bags of her belongings as she prepared to go to Millie's door. Hazel purposely left all of Seven's gifts to her in his house, not wanting to take them with her. Seven had hurt her feelings so bad and Hazel couldn't understand how Seven could be so cold to her after they had established such a close bond. Her hands began to shake, feeling scared and lonely without Seven. She had been depending on him for the past few months and without him she felt inadequate. If he knew it or not, he was her strength and now without him she was weak.

"I'm so sorry, Seven," Hazel whispered as she didn't fully understand why he shunned her. Hazel stepped out of the car and headed to Millie's.

Millie sat at her kitchen table with a belt wrapped tightly around her arm and a needle in her hand. She had just gotten a free pack from Rico and although she didn't want to take it, she did; giving into the temptation. Although she had flushed Mouse's pack down the toilet, minutes later she had stumbled upon a free pack of dope. It seemed inevitable for her to shoot dope into her veins on that given day. It was as if the pack that Li'l Rico had given her was a special pack when Millie saw it. It was neatly packed and a red rubber band was around it, as if the pack was calling her name with a golden ticket to ecstasy. She set the needle down and smacked her arm trying to get a vein to show. After a couple of smacks a big, green vein presented itself and Millie picked up the needle. She placed it to her skin, almost piercing it, and . . . Knock, knock, knock.

"Damn," Millie whispered as she was interrupted. She quickly put her needle under a towel that sat on the table and unwrapped her arm. She stormed to the door and found Hazel on the other side, holding a bag. She had tear-filled eyes.

"Hazelnut, what's wrong?" she asked as her irritated frown formed into a concerned look.

"He doesn't want me anymore," Hazel said as she broke down right then and there, crying.

"Come in, baby," Millie said as she opened her arms, welcoming Hazel. Hazel fell into Millie's arms and hugged her tightly.

"He thinks you set him up. That guy Mouse came and tried . . ." Hazel said, trying to get the words out before she began to hyperventilate.

"Shh. Calm down. I would never do that," Millie lied, not wanting to admit what she had done.

"I know. I tried to tell him that you would never do anything like that but he wouldn't listen."

"Well, you know you have a home right here. Fuck that nigga. You got me," Millie said as she guided Hazel in and onto the couch. Millie walked to the door and got Hazel's bag and put it in the room. "Your room is just like you left it. Don't worry about it," Millie said as she walked back into the living room and took a seat next to Hazel, throwing her arm around her and caressing her as Hazel cried on her shoulder.

It hurt Millie, knowing that she was the cause of the domino effect that left Hazel miserable. Millie instantly wanted to make Hazel feel better.

"Hazel, you just need to give him a little time to cool off. That man loves you. Men are like that; when they get mad they push everything and everybody away. When emotions enter . . . reason leaves," Millie said, dropping jewels to the young girl who cried in her arms.

"He didn't seem like he was just mad. He looked at me like he hated me," Hazel said as she looked at Millie, wiping the tears from her cheeks.

"Just give him a little time. He'll come around, watch. Tell you what. How about I go to the store and get some of that banana split ice cream that you love so much. Shit . . . ice cream always makes me feel better," Millie joked, trying to get Hazel to smile. Hazel wasn't smiling but Millie was determined to change that. Millie smiled, knowing that she finally had gotten her girl back. Millie quickly got up and put on her jacket as she headed for the door. She slipped on her house shoes while exiting. She was so into helping Hazel, she had forgotten about shooting the dope. Millie smiled as she walked out of the apartment, feeling so good that Hazel was back around. It seemed as if Millie's spirits were instantly lifted.

***

Only minutes after Millie left, Hazel cried as she put the belt in her mouth, jerking her neck so that she could tighten it around her arm. The pain and sorrow that Seven caused her drove her to surrender herself to dope once again. "I loved you, Seven. How could you?" she mumbled out of her clenched teeth. She took the laced heroin-filled needle that Millie had left on the table, and carefully injected it into her vein. The drug slowly crept up her vein like a snake in a field of grass. Instantly Hazel's eyes rolled in the back of her head and the good feeling that she had missed for so long re-emerged, giving her a relaxed and orgasmic feeling. That feeling soon became a burning, painful one as foam began to volcano through her mouth and a drip of blood came from her left eye. Hazel's body jerked wildly and she fell out of the chair, landing on the hardwood floor while beginning to go into convulsions and shaking violently. Sadly, she was experiencing her untimely death.

In the last moments of her life, she stopped shaking and had a quiet, calm experience as she thought back to a time when she was a little girl. She thought about Apple and how he described New York in the dead of winter and how beautiful it was. She imagined herself walking through a park with an all-white mink coat on, walking toward a bridge. She looked back at Apple, who was admiring the mime do his precise and astonishing act. Hazel then imagined herself climbing onto a bridge's rail and holding her arms out like a bird as the cold New York weather flowed through her fingers. Just before Hazel took her last breath in reality, she jumped off the bridge in the scene playing out in her mind; flying free as a bird. Hazel was finally free. She was finally at a place where she would experience no more pain, no more heartbreak, and no more addiction. She took her last breath and then stared aimlessly into space with her eyes wide open. Hazel Brown was dead.

Millie came through the door smiling, about to tell Hazel how she was going to start Insight the next day. Hazel was her motivation to get clean for good.

"I was thinking, I'ma really do it this time," Millie said, coming in with a bag full of goodies for them to eat. Millie was so busy talking and putting down the bags she didn't see Hazel on the floor with her eyes open, staring into space, and lifeless.

"Hazel! They didn't have banana split so I got strawberry. Naw, I'm lying . . . I like strawberry and only had enough to buy one pint!" Millie yelled, thinking Hazel had gone in the back and couldn't hear her. "Hazel," she yelled again, but this time turning around. Millie looked down and saw Hazel sprawled out on the floor with the needle in her arm.

"Hazel? No, no, no," Millie said as she looked at the syringe sticking out of her forearm. Then Millie looked at Hazel's eyes and saw that she wasn't blinking . . . or breathing. "Hazel!" Millie yelled as her heart dropped into her stomach. The blood drained from Millie's face as she felt like she couldn't breathe. She quickly dropped to her knees and cradled Hazel's head. Millie shook Hazel and tried to give her CPR, but it was to no avail; she had gone to the other side. "Noooooooo!" Millie cried as she wept with her dead Hazelnut in her arms, rocking back and forth, holding her baby.

Chapter Twenty-two

Six days later a small memorial service was held for Hazel. Millie, along with a couple friends of Hazel from the Insight Center, attended. The entire Insight staff was also present and some of its patients were there to celebrate the life of their fallen peer. Millie sat in the back row inside the church, struggling with the loss of her only loved one and also the pains of heroin withdrawal. Millie had cried for the past week straight and when she found out that Hazel died because of rat poisoning, she instantly knew that it was meant for her. The guilt of knowing that she was responsible for killing her baby Hazel weighed heavy on her soul and revenge was number one on her priority list. She knew that she had to go to see Rico to get answers, but for now she had to bury her love, Hazel. Millie was expecting to see Seven there, but he never showed. Little did she know, Seven was also overwhelmed with guilt. He had ordered the death of Millie, but killed Hazel instead.

While Millie cried in the back, the doors of the church opened and all eyes went to the man with the apple mark on his face. It was not guessing; everyone knew it was Hazel's father, Apple. He was escorted by two uniformed guards and he was still handcuffed as he made his way down the aisle, teary-eyed and hesitant. Although his eyes were watery, his face had a look of rage. Apple knew that his daughter had been slipped a hot shot from Rah, and Seven was the cause of it.

Apple slowly approached the casket; he stopped just short of his daughter and looked at the guards. "Come on, fellas. Show my baby girl some respect," Apple whispered. In so many words, Apple requested the guards to let him see his daughter's body without being escorted by authorities. The guards looked at each other and agreed to grant Apple's wishes. Apple slowly walked up to the casket and looked at his angel, lying there, breathless. She barely looked like herself. Her face seemed as if it were hard as stone and she had a smug expression on her face with heavy makeup on. The tears began to flow as Apple's hands and knees shook uncontrollably.

"I'm so sorry, baby. I'm so sorry. It's all my fault. I should have never left you. It's . . . all . . . my fault," he said, breaking down and burying his face in his hands. He bent down and kissed his daughter's forehead. Apple gave her a long kiss goodnight and turned and walked toward the exit; he couldn't stand it anymore. He couldn't stay and watch Hazel get put in the ground, so he decided to say his good-byes at that point and not stay for the entire ceremony. Just as he got to the last row he felt a hand pick up his. It was Millie.

"Apple," she whispered with tear-filled eyes. "I'm Millie," she whispered as she looked deep into his eyes. "I was there . . ." Millie said just before Apple put his finger on his lip, signaling her to stop talking.

"Come see me," he simply said as he gently pulled his hand away from her and exited. He knew that Millie was there with Hazel at the time of her death, and he wanted to talk to her to ask her about his only daughter's last breaths.

Apple walked out of the courthouse and he saw a tinted truck. Somehow he knew it was Seven.

Seven sat in his truck solo, with watery eyes, not having the courage to pay his respects to Hazel, knowing he was the cause of her untimely demise. He watched Apple coming out of the church and his heart dropped, not knowing what to say to his mentor. How could he explain that he accidently killed Hazel? How? Seven clenched his jaws tightly and stared at Apple coming toward him. Apple looked at the window as if he was staring straight at Seven. Seven's heart began to beat rapidly and he saw Apple quickly break loose from the two officers and rush to the car.

"Seven! Seven!" Apple yelled, approaching the car. Seven rolled down his window, exposing his pained face.

"Apple," Seven said, trying to explain that it was an accident. Apple finally approached the car breathing heavily, while the guards were rushing to get him.

"Seven, how could you? I raised you! I held you down and this how you repay me? I asked you to protect my baby, not kill her!" Apple yelled as white film formed in the corner of his mouth while tears flowed. Seven tried to say something but nothing came out. As the guards approached Apple, they grabbed him and put him in the handcuffs, but Apple never took that sinister stare off of Seven. Just before the officers pulled him away, he spit into Seven's face. "I hate you nigga! I made you!" Apple yelled as he got forcefully pulled away and stuffed into the backseat of the police car.

Seven slowly wiped the spit off of his face and gripped the pistol that sat on his lap. He could have busted Apple for disrespecting him, but he couldn't. Seven was so hurt that his hero had just told him that he hated him. His Superman had just been taken away from him. Seven had never been so heartbroken in his life. Nothing he could do could right his wrong and he would have to live with Hazel's death on his shoulder forever. Seven shook his head from side to side and watched as the police car pulled away. Things would never be the same. Seven breathed heavily and a single tear rolled down his cheek and onto his gun. "I'm sorry, Hazel. I never meant this to happen to you," he whispered to himself as he started up the car. The single event had just turned him cold. He quickly channeled his pain into anger. Seven waited in his car for over an hour and waited to see the funeral workers act as pallbearers and escort Hazel's casket out.

The sight was overwhelming for Seven and he released a rare tear, hurting inside out. He pulled off as the men began to toss the dirt over her casket. He couldn't stand the sight, knowing that he was the cause of it. Seven thought about killing Millie, but he knew that it wouldn't do any good. What was the use of killing a dopefiend? Seven wished he had been thinking like that a week earlier. If he had been, Hazel would have still been alive.

***

Millie watched as they threw dirt on Hazel's casket. Millie knew that a piece of her had died that day and she was determined to make some-one pay. All the sorrow she had been feeling the past week was slowly altering into anger. Millie gripped her aching stomach as the withdrawal pains made it almost impossible to stand, but she stood tall for Hazel. Millie had vowed to never put another drug in her body. Her drug use and influence had made a beautiful girl's life end far too soon. Millie knew that it was she who was supposed to be getting buried rather than Hazel and that was the hardest thing for her to accept. The fact that she started Hazel on the drugs made it that much worse. Millie was about to make someone pay. The old Millie was dead and she was determined to get to the bottom of the situation. First, she knew that she would have to go and see Apple, giving him an explanation.

Chapter Twenty-three

"I'm about to cum!" the woman yelled as she bent over the chair with her legs parted widely. She was totally nude, except for the six-inch heels that she wore at Mouse's request. Mouse watched the rippling effect in the woman's behind as he stroked her from the back at a rapid pace. Mouse was sweating heavily and the sex was so good that it had him lightheaded and wobbly.

"This is so good," he whispered as he gradually slowed down, feeling faint. "Damn," he mumbled, never having sex that made him feel so woozy. Little did he know it wasn't the sex that had him feeling tired; it was the pill that Toya had secretly slipped into his drink. Seven and Rah had convinced Toya to take one for the team and set Mouse up. At first, Toya was irate that Rah would ask her to have sex with another man, but the $25,000 that Seven had placed in her hand made her see things their way real quick.

Mouse's strokes got slower and slower until he eventually collapsed on Toya's back, totally blacking out.

Mouse's head was banging from an excruciating headache as he came to. His vision was blurry and the sun crept through the hotel's blinds. *Damn, I been out since last night?* Mouse thought as he attempted to wipe the sleep out of his eye. He never got a chance to raise his hand to his face because he was roped and bound to a chair in the center of the hotel room. *What the fuck?*

Mouse thought as his vision became clear. He tried to scream, but no sound escaped his mouth because of the duct tape wrapped tightly around his lips. He looked down and saw that he was tied up, not having any room to maneuver. It wasn't until moments later that Mouse noticed the figure standing in front of him with a bandaged head and a cane; it was Seven. Seven was standing, waiting patiently for Mouse to regain his consciousness.

"Rise and shine," Seven said coldly as he sat down in his wheelchair that was directly behind him. Seven grimaced as the pain shot through the right side of his body. It had been an entire month since he had been shot and he anticipated the day that he would see Mouse again. That day had come. Mouse was completely baffled and couldn't believe who he was looking at. He was sure that he had murdered Seven at his apartment.

"Oh, that bitch woke up, huh?" Rah said as he emerged from the bathroom, wiping his hands dry. Seven nodded his head as he never took his eyes off of Mouse. Mouse began to sweat and his heart rate sped up. He knew what time it was and karma was knocking at his front door. Seven looked at Rah and threw his head in the direction of Mouse, and Rah immediately walked over and gave him a hard punch to the eye. Mouse squirmed and cringed as the pain overwhelmed him. Rah laid another one on him, but that time he hit him in the other eye. That punch split Mouse's upper cheekbone wide open, causing blood to trickle down his face. The sounds of Mouse's whimpers and heavy breathing filled the room. Rah took off his shirt, displaying his chiseled physique and tattooed body. He was about to go to work on Mouse and didn't want to mess up his silk Cavalli shirt that he just purchased. He neatly laid it on the bed and focused back on Mouse. Rah gave him repeated blows to the head, swelling him up beyond recognition. The vicious beating continued for fifteen minutes, before Seven finally spoke up.

"That's enough, fam," he said. Rah was breathing heavily and sweating as if he just ran the New York City Marathon. Rah gave Mouse another punch to the mid-section for good measure before he walked away. Seven rolled the wheelchair up to Mouse and quickly ripped off the duct tape from Mouse's mouth, causing vomit to gush out and onto Mouse's chest.

"Ma . . . man, don't kill me. It was all business. You know how the game go," Mouse said, trying to get out of the sticky situation. "It didn't even supposed to go down like that!" Mouse said, half crying.

"Is that right?' Seven asked calmly as he pulled out a weed-filled cigar and lit it. Seven usually didn't smoke, but he had developed the habit over the past couple of weeks, being that it helped him deal with the pain on the left side of his body. After Seven took a deep pull off of his cigar, he blew the thick smoke directly in Mouse's face. Seven then pulled a gun that was tucked in his waist and set it on his lap.

"Please, Seven. Please don't shoot me," Mouse pleaded as he stared at the chrome on Seven's lap.

"Don't shoot you?" Seven questioned as he grinned, not believing the audacity of Mouse. "I'm not going to shoot you, my nigga. You are not even worth the bullet. But I can tell you what I am going to do," Seven said nonchalantly, as if he were engrossed in casual conversation between gentlemen. Seven paused. He was absolutely enjoying the pained look on Mouse's face. Mouse instantly grew more terrified and couldn't control himself. A stream of piss ran down his leg as fear set in. He saw Rah step up with a syringe in his hand. Rah squirted the little bit of water that was at the tip of the syringe and held it up in the air showing the brown, watery substance that it contained.

"I know you're wondering what's in that syringe, huh? Let me help you out. You probably were thinking it's *Lady Luck*, right? Nah, fuck that. This is a special blend made especially for you, Mouse. That's battery acid mixed with rat poison," Seven said as he grinned again and took another pull of the cigar.

"Ooo wee. This shit is about to hurt like a mufucka," Rah said jokingly as he waited for the green light from Seven.

"Hell yeah. I'm glad I'm not this nigga," Seven said as him and Rah exchanged smiles. Seven then blew the weed smoke out slowly.

"Please, please don't kill me. I got a daughter, man," Mouse pleaded as he tried to wiggle himself out of the rope but it was no use.

"I know. Li'l Tasha, right? Live right off of Harriet Street with your baby mama. Pretty little girl. I'll be going to see her a little bit later this afternoon. I'll be sending her to the exact place you're going. Don't worry," Seven said, meaning every word. He had no sympathy whatsoever and Mouse had started a domino effect that had made Seven cold as ice, borderline isane. He didn't give a fuck anymore. The doctor that performed Seven's surgery, removing the bullet, said that the bullet struck a nerve that alters the brain's emotional side and a person's compassion. Boy, was he right. Now Seven was cold-blooded as ever. Rah wrapped a belt tightly around Mouse's arm and smacked his forearm, waiting on a good vein to form. When it did, he jammed the syringe in and emptied all of the content into Mouse's bloodstream, giving him one of the most painful deaths a man could experience. Mouse screamed at the top of his lungs and the acid ate away at his skin and caused him to go into a painful convulsion while throwing up blood. He shook vigorously, just as Hazel had done. Mouse suffered tremendously as his complexion turned from light brown to a beet red as his arms had swollen to three times their original size. Seven and Rah passed the cigar back and forth causally, while watching Mouse suffer to death.

Seven left the hotel room, alongside Rah, with a different attitude and a new perspective on life. One would think that Seven would leave the drug game alone, but he was about to go harder than ever before. He would never let anyone get close enough to hurt him. He was about to become like a ghost to the streets and never be accessible again. He had come up with this master plan while sitting back mourning the death of Hazel and rehabilitating his injury. He was about to become untouchable.

He had no one except Rah and tainted memories of what love eventually did to a person: caused pain. He had truly understood the meaning of the saying "Love is pain and pain is love" firsthand.

Li'l Rico stood on his usual post as he waited for his first dope sale of the day. He wore an all-black oversized hoodie with both of his hands tucked inside of his pockets as he scoped down the block. He gripped his .25 in his hand as he concealed it and waited patiently. Just as he thought he saw a dopefiend straggling down the block, he took a deeper look, and he noticed that it was Millie. He hadn't seen her since he gave her the laced pack of dope. He had heard about what happened to Hazel and felt bad for what he helped do, but he couldn't worry about it too much because that's how the game went sometimes. He watched as Millie walked toward him, scratching her arms and jonesing badly. Her lips were chapped and her hair was wild and all over her head.

"What this bitch want?" he asked himself as he saw her coming directly toward him.

"Li'l Rico! Li'l Rico! Hook me up, baby," Millie begged as she had a sad look in her eye. Rico smacked his lips and couldn't believe that Millie still wanted dope from him after he had given her a laced pack. "Dopeheads will do anything to get high," he said under his breath as she approached him.

"Li'l Rico, I'm hurting real bad. I really need a pack to shake the kinks off," Millie begged as she scratched her arms vigorously.

"Look, I didn't know that pack was bad," Li'l Rico said, disregarding her request for dope, wanting to get the guilt off of his chest in some way. If Millie forgave him, at least he would feel better about what had happened.

"Don't worry about it. I know Seven's people gave it to you. Everyone knows that. It wasn't your fault," Millie said as she shifted from side to side and gripped her stomach and grunted because of the pain.

"For real?" Li'l Rico asked, feeling better already.

"Yeah, it's cool," Millie answered as she looked around, fidgeting.

"Yo', here you go. This one's on the house," Li'l Rico said as he reached into his pocket and pulled out a pack for Millie.

"Are you serious?" Millie asked as she grew a surprised look on her face. She lit up like a kid on Christmas morning.

"Yeah, it's the least I can do," Li'l Rico answered. Millie took the pack and then smiled at him.

"I know ain't shit in this world free. So, let me suck your dick for you, okay? I'll do it real good, too. Deal?" Millie said, not wanting Rico to feel like she owed him something. Rico wanted to say no, knowing that Millie had robbed him before, but his soldier in his pants began to tingle. Millie pulled out one of her breasts and flashed it at him, knowing it would drive his young hormones crazy. "Come on. Let me earn this pack," Millie said as she rubbed her dark brown nipple. Rico scanned the block to see if anyone was looking and decided to grant Millie's wish.

"Let's go over there," Rico said, pointing to the alley.

"Bet," Millie answered as she hurried over and immediately dropped to her knees. Rico followed her over and immediately whipped out his rod to let Millie please him. Rico threw his head back, anticipating the great sensation that Millie's lips had to offer.

After a couple of seconds of not feeling anything wet wrapped around his pole, Rico opened his eyes and looked down. What he saw almost made him piss on himself. Millie had a four-inch blade in one hand and his erect rod in her other, looking up at him.

"Whoa! Hold up!" Rico said as he froze in fear as Millie's facial expression had totally changed. At first she looked like a woman in pain from withdrawal, but that look had been a front. She now had a fire in her eyes that screamed revenge. She was thirsty for payback. Millie hadn't touched a drug in weeks, since Hazel's funeral. She had gone cold turkey and forced herself to be drug free. It was very difficult, but she did it. She had finally emerged from the darkness to seek revenge in Hazel's name.

"Don't move or I will chop this mufucka off. Try me if you wanna," Millie whispered harshly as she stood to her feet, still having his penis gripped tightly. She had pressed the blade to the side of it, making a tiny trickle of blood run onto her fingers. Li'l Rico was sweating bullets as he breathed lightly and blinked his eyes feverishly. Li'l Rico thought about reaching for his gun, but he didn't want to take the chance of having his manhood chopped off. Millie saw the expression on Li'l Rico's face as if he was contemplating something, so she looked down and saw the bulge of the gun through his hoodie. She swiftly reached into his pocket, pulling out the gun, leaving the knife in his pocket. She did it so fast that Li'l Rico couldn't even react. Once again he was staring down the barrel of his own gun.

"Why did you do it? Why? "Millie asked as she flipped the gun off of safety, knowing exactly how to handle a gun.

"It wasn't me, I swear," Li'l Rico pleaded. "Rah slipped me the pack and told me to give it to you. People in the streets were saying that you helped Mouse set up Seven to get killed," Rico said with fear evident in his voice and his hands out in front of him as if it could block the bullets. Millie had heard all she needed to hear. She let off a round in Rico's forehead, causing a loud blast to echo throughout the alley. Li'l Rico dropped instantly. She walked over his body and watched as he struggled for air and blood leaked from the right side of his mouth. Without hesitation, she let off two more rounds into his chest, rocking him to sleep forever. Her hands shook but she didn't regret what she had done. Millie was on a mission. Now she wanted Rah dead, since she thought Seven had already been killed.

Millie sat in the chair and looked across the table where Apple was waiting for her. Apple's eyes were red and his beard was scraggily as if he hadn't shaved in weeks. He took his time sitting down and stared at Millie for a while before picking up the phone. Apple's eyes didn't have the same glare that they once had. He had bags under his eyes and had lost a little weight in a six-week period. It was six weeks to the day since Hazel had been murdered. He finally picked up the phone and looked at Millie.

"Speak," he said as if Millie were nothing.

"I'm Millie, and . . ." Millie said, wanting to introduce herself, knowing that Apple had never seen her except for at the funeral.

"I know who you are, Milian Summers. Originally from Baltimore. Used to run with Tical

Manny, right?" Apple said, on point with his information.

"Yeah, how you know?" Millie said, surprised that Apple had known so much even though he was behind bars.

"I have my ways of finding out things. You were with my baby when . . ." Apple paused, beginning to tear up. "When she died?"

Millie shamefully nodded her head and dropped it. Flashes of that horrible day began to form in her thoughts and created an empty feeling inside of her chest. "Yes, I was. The pack she hit was laced," Millie said, not even looking into Apple's eyes. She was afraid of what she might see. She, herself, had felt like she had lost a daughter, but she knew that her feelings wouldn't and couldn't compare to Apple's. "I know who did it. It was—"

"Close your mouth," Apple said sternly as he knocked on the glass, trying to get Millie to look up at him. "I know who did it. I knew who did it a couple of days after it happened. News travels fast in here," he said. Apple knew that it was a possibility that their conversation was being monitored, so he wanted to leave out names.

"But how did . . ." Millie started to say.

"Never mind that!" Apple said, reining his tone slightly. "Let's just get to business, okay?"

Apple said, wanting to cut straight to the chase. Tears formed in his eyes and he couldn't stop them from falling and his nose began to run. He looked desperate.

"I left Hazel some money. I was . . . I was going to give it to her when she got clean. But now I can't. I want you to have it and do whatever it takes to get the man responsible for my baby's death. Put it on his head in the streets. Contract for his murder."

Millie remained silent, nodding in agreement at Apple's instructions. "Do you know where my old house is at? The one Hazel grew up in," Apple said, knowing the authorities knew nothing about the home he owned. He gave it to Ms. Johnson when he got put away, putting it in her name.

"Yeah, I know where it's at," Millie confirmed, remembering when Hazel showed her the boarded-up house she grew up in. Hazel didn't have the money to keep it up and was so into drugs that she let the city take claim to it because of back taxes.

"It's underneath the doghouse. I want you to give me your word that you will get him," Apple said just before with an intense glare. "I know that pack was meant for you. I know! Now it is your duty to do this for my baby!"

"You have my word."

"I also want you to go see my friend," Apple said as he reached into his pocket and pulled out a piece of paper that had Hassan's address and number on it. He slid it through the opening at the bottom of the thick glass and Millie grabbed it, quickly putting it in her purse. Apple had clout throughout the jail system, so the guard turned the other way when the exchange was made.

"Tell him to cut Seven off. He will understand," Apple said.

With that, he hung up the phone and got up and left, not wanting to talk to Millie anymore. He knew that Millie used dope with his daughter and he hated Millie for that. For now, Millie was nothing but a pawn for Apple to seek revenge on Seven. Millie thought Seven was dead, but she soon would find out.

"Lights off!" The sound of the husky corrections officer sounded throughout the halls as the lights shut off. Apple lay in his bed smiling and laughing out loud as tears fell from his eyes, thinking about how he and Hazel would sit up and have fun, just the two of them sharing happy times. She was his pride and joy and the thought of her smile brought brief joy to his heart. But the joy was instantly taken away when he thought about her death. Apple put on a forced smile as he clasped his hands on his chest and closed his eyes, wanting to go to sleep thinking about the good times.

Two hours later Apple was sound asleep and in a deep dream. The images in his head were so vivid and clear, creating a theatrical-type movie in his thoughts. He walked with his arm around Hazel in a New York park. He looked down at her and smiled. In his dream she was still a little girl, smiling while rocking the expensive mink he had purchased for her. "I love you, Daddy," Hazel said as she looked up at him and smiled from ear to ear.

"I love you too, Hazel. With all my heart," he said as he spotted a mime doing an act just a few yards from them.

"Ooh look, Daddy!" Hazel screamed as she also spotted the mime. She looked up at Apple and asked, "Can we stop and watch please?" she asked, getting more excited with each word.

"Of course," he said as he playfully thumped the tip of her nose, making her giggle in enjoyment. Hazel released Apple's arm and ran to the mime as he pretended as if he was stepping out of a gigantic box. His movements were so precise and perfect. Hazel was standing there, clapping in admiration and jumping up and down. Apple watched as he smiled, feeling happy because his favorite girl was happy. He slowly walked towards them, his gators clicking against the pavement, and a long trench over his shoulders. He wore an all-white suit with diamond cufflinks to set it off. A toothpick hung out of his mouth and he was looking like a gangster, just as he would like it. Apple joined them and stood beside Hazel as she continued to watch. He took another glance at Hazel; however, she had grown into an adult. She was a tad taller and had red lipstick on now. She still was beautiful and still enjoying the show. She leaned over and pecked him on the cheek.

"Thanks, Daddy," she whispered. Apple remained silent and just smiled, responding to her with just that gesture. Apple focused his attention back on the mime and observed his movements. Right before his eyes, the mime mystically turned into Hassan, his dope connect.

"Hello, my friend. We are about to get rich," Hassan said as he showed Apple a duffle bag full of bricks of heroin. Apple frowned as he tried to understand what had happened, not understanding that he was in a dream. His mind was playing tricks on him. He looked at the bricks in the bag and temporarily got distracted.

He looked next to himself and noticed that Hazel was gone.

"Hazel? Where are you, baby girl?" he called, looking for her, doing a total three-sixty searching for her. It wasn't until he looked up the way, did he see his baby on top of the ledge that was over the water. Her nice mink was all of a sudden covered in blood. Apple frowned, trying to make sure his eyes weren't playing tricks on him. He squinted his eyes and stepped toward the bridge.

"Hazel!" he yelled as he watched her take off her bloody coat and let it drop into the water. "Hazel! Get down!" he yelled as she took one look at him and smiled with a lost look in her eyes. She spread her arms out like an eagle and looked down at the water. Apple could see the tracks in her arms from using heroin and that sight alone made his chief feel hollow with guilt. Apple took off full speed trying to get her, but before he could make it . . . she leaped.

"Noooooo! Nooooooo!" he yelled as he ran to the ledge and looked down frantically trying to locate his baby girl. "Hazel!" he yelled as he began to cry, scanning the waves, trying to find Hazel. Nevertheless, he only saw the mink coat coasting away, slowly coasting on top of the waves. He looked back where Hassan was originally standing and noticed that he had disappeared. Apple was now in the park alone. Apple's dream was symbolic for the failed life that he felt he had lived. He was too busy focusing on the money and he let Hazel slip away from him in his dream . . . just like he did in real life. Apple had abandoned Hazel by going to jail. He felt a sharp pain go through his heart and gripped the left side of his chest. In his dream, he was dying . . . The sad thing was that he was dying in real life also. Apple fell over the cliff and followed Hazel to the bottom of the ocean, where they would be together forever. He was finally reunited with his baby and no prison or drug could ever tear them apart again. "I love you, Daddy," Hazel whispered in his ear as they both slowly fell to the bottom of the ocean in each other's arms.

Apple suffered from a heart attack at 3:15 that morning and never woke up. He was pronounced dead at the age of thirty-nine in his sleep. He was found dead in his cot. The doctors said he died of a massive heart attack, but anyone who knew Apple well, knew that he really died of a broken heart.

Chapter Twenty-four

Millie was covered in dirt as she dug with the steel shovel. She sweated as she frantically searched for the package that Apple had told her about in his backyard. It was the end of winter and the weather had warmed up, a good thing for Millie. She wiped the sweat from her eyebrow and dug the shovel into the ground once again, but that time she hit something hard, causing a loud ping sound. Millie quickly dropped to her knees, tossed the shovel, and began to dig hurriedly with both of her hands. Just as Apple said, there was something there. A small chest with flowers on it appeared. Millie dug around the box some more and finally pulled it out. She quickly unsnapped the latch and looked inside. Stacks of fifty- and hundred-dollar bills were wrapped in Ziploc bags. Millie's eyes shot wide open and instantly her arm began to tingle, a natural reaction to a recovering addict: money equated to copping dope. Millie quickly shook off the urge and the voice of Apple sounded throughout her head. "I know that pack was meant for you!" Millie grabbed the money and stuffed it in the book bag she had nearby. She was about to put her plan in motion. Millie had a one-way trip back to her hometown on the east coast. She was about to get herself together and bring the old Millie back. She knew that without power she would never be able to touch Seven. Seven was much too smart to make the same mistake twice and Millie fully understood that. Flint knew Millie as nothing more than a dopefiend, but what they didn't know was that she was one of the baddest and biggest that ever graced this ill-willed Earth. Millie was about to go back to her roots and come back full force. She understood that Seven was a boss . . . and to kill a boss you have to be a boss. Simple blueprint to the game that Millie fully comprehended. She was taught by the best.

Seven and Rah drove down the interstate while Nas lightly pumped out of the speakers, both of them slowly nodding their heads in unison enjoying the melody. Seven had just gotten word that Apple died in his sleep while in jail, and although Apple hated him at the time of his death, Seven still had love for him. Seven looked in his rearview and checked to see if Toya was still following him, with the car full of dope. He used her as his mule, knowing that a woman was always less likely to get pulled over and be subjected to a search. Seven was on his way back from a brief road trip. He had gone to meet his Ohio dope connect to re-up. Hassan had cut him off at the request of Apple, so Seven went back to getting his dope from elsewhere. Luckily Rah had family in Ohio who was getting it and that's how Seven made that connection. It worked out in Seven's favor because his new connect had better dope with dirt-cheap prices.

Seven grabbed the spliff from the ashtray and took a deep pull. He kept having visions of himself getting shot by Mouse and that heightened his paranoia to the point where he developed a sweaty hands problem. Seven passed the spliff to his right. Rah grabbed the spliff and reached to the dash to turn down the radio.

"Fam, you okay?" Rah said, noticing the expression on Seven's face.

"Yeah, I'm good. Why you say that?" Seven asked.

"I don't know. Something is just different about you lately. You smoking now and before you never would touch any drugs. You are always in your own little world. You just seem spaced out sometimes. This ain't you, fam," Rah said as he took a deep pull of the spliff, letting a little smoke escape his mouth just before he sucked it back in deep into his lungs.

"I just got a whole new perspective on life now. I don't give a fuck no more. I don't have anybody but you, my nigga," Seven said sincerely. Both men took in what was said and like only gangster would, they didn't discuss it any further. There was pain in Seven's voice and the deaths of Hazel and now Apple were weighing heavy on his heart. Seven was transforming into another person. Mouse fucked it up for everybody. If Seven had respect in the street before, now he was about to make himself feared. He now understood that fear was more powerful than respect. Because if Mouse feared him, the robbery would have never happened. Now Seven was more ruthless, more strategic, and eventually he would become untouchable. This was the making of a kingpin.

Millie had just left Apple's grave and left flowers on the site. Although she didn't know Apple well, she felt it was right. She also visited Hazel's gravesite and paid her respects to her baby. Now, the only thing on her mind was making Seven pay. She had camped out in front of Seven's apartment all day to only find out that he had been moved out. She had no idea where to start looking for Seven so she hit the block with a plan.

Millie walked into the dope house with a book bag on her back. The hustlers and some of the fiends began to look at Millie funny, not expecting to see her because of her extended absence from the underworld.

"Is that Millie?" an older man said just before he smacked his neck, trying to find a vein.

"Millie?" another fiend called out, but Millie wasn't there to socialize. She had business to handle as she walked over to the table where four young hustlers sat. Millie approached the table and held the straps of the book bag tightly.

"Yo, can I talk to you all for a minute?" she asked. It seemed as if Millie didn't even say anything because the hustlers ignored her request as they sat around talking shit among each other.

"Excuse me!" Millie said louder this time, demanding their attention. All eyes shot to her and one hustler grew a smug look on his face when he noticed who it was. There was a rumor that Millie had killed Li'l Rico, but he quickly dismissed the notion when he thought about who she was in his eyes: nothing more than a junkie. But little did he know, Millie was fully capable of murder and would be willing to do it again if the situation arose. She was out for revenge.

"Oh shit! It's Millie," one of the hustlers said as he looked her up and down, remembering how she gave him the best sex he had ever had a while back.

"Damn, it sholl is," a hustler agreed as he noticed that Millie had gained a little weight, which made her look more healthy.

"I need to holler at y'all for real," Millie said, growing impatient.

"Yo, what up?" the hustler asked.

"Let's go in the back," Millie said as she headed to the rear of the dope house. The hustlers all looked at each other, thinking Millie wanted them to run a train on her in trade for dope, but she had another thing in mind. Millie waited in the room as three of the four hustlers came in, smiling.

"I got a proposition for all of you," Millie said, looking each one of them in the eye. The men instantly began to unbutton their pants but Millie quickly took off the book bag and exposed the bag full of money, catching them all off guard. "It's eighty thousand dollars in here," Millie said as she kneeled down and placed the bag on the floor. She looked up to see their surprised facial expressions.

"What the fuck? Where you get that shit from, Millie?" one of the hustlers asked.

"Look, don't worry about it. I need somebody killed. Someone I can't get close to . . . feel me? That's why I need you niggas to do it for me."

"Fuck yeah! Where that nigga at?" one hustler asked as he began to lick his lips and rub his hands together as he stared at the money as if it were steak.

"It's Seven," Millie said, and noticed all of their expressions had suddenly changed.

"Seven? Big homie Seven? You got to be out of your fucking mind," one hustler said as he thought about how Seven had tortured and killed Mouse for trying to cross him.

"And even if we wanted to do it for you, we couldn't. Ever since Mouse popped him, he doesn't even show his face around here anymore. Nobody hasn't seen him in a long while. He don't fuck with the hood no more, just supplies it," one hustler said as he broke down Seven's new habits.

They all wanted no part of it. All of them automatically began to think about robbing the brave woman in front of them. Millie looked at the others and they were all singing the same song, so she zipped up her bag and stood up.

"Scary-ass niggas," she whispered as she headed out. She saw one of the hustlers slide his hand near his waist as if he was about to pull a gun. Millie wasn't green to the game; she anticipated them having the urge to rob her, because they looked at her as nothing more than a junkie. She quickly pulled out a gun that was inside the book bag, surprising them all, and walked backward toward the door. They never expected Millie to have a gun, but they didn't know Millie's past. She used to hold court in the streets of Baltimore and knew how to handle situations like that one accordingly.

"Don't think about it," she warned. "I tried to put y'all down but I see Seven got all of you shook. Y'all can get it too," she promised as she faded into the front room and quickly headed out and ran to an alley off of the block. Millie had to approach the situation from another angle. She understood that Seven had secluded himself and would be hard to touch. But she promised herself that vengeance would be sought. But first, she was to return to Baltimore and get herself together and next time she would come correct.

Millie sat Indian style in the dirt next to Hazel's grave and talked to her as if she were still alive. To a bystander, it would look as if Millie had gone crazy, but Millie didn't care; she was talking to her Hazelnut. Millie stood up and walked directly in front of the tombstone. She kissed her fingertips and then rubbed the stone that had Hazel's name engraved in it. Millie quickly wiped away the tear that fell, smiled, and walked away. She was going back to see Apple to get his advice on getting to Seven.

Chapter Twenty-five

Millie left the correctional facility in disbelief, just getting the news that Apple had died in his sleep a few weeks back. The doctors said he died from a heart attack, but Millie knew the real cause of death was from a father's grief. Millie had no alliance and would have to get Seven on her own. After an hour drive back to Flint, she pulled up to her home and grabbed the book bag full of money that sat in her passenger's side. She got out and looked at the setting sun, which gave the sky a purple hue. She took a deep breath and headed to her door. Once Millie approached her doorstep, she got a funny feeling for some reason. Something didn't seem right. She stopped in her tracks just before she put the key in the keyhole. She heard movement inside of her apartment and quickly stepped away from the door and reached into the book bag where the gun was tucked. Millie heard a gun cock from the inside of her house and she instinctively took off running to the car, knowing that Seven had sent someone to finish the job. She frantically jumped in the car and started it up, but the sound of shots thumping the metal on the car made her pause and duck for cover.

"Aw shit!" she yelled as glass shattered onto her head and the sounds of bullets whizzing by her head erupted. Knowing that she had to get out of there fast, she threw the car into drive trying to get away from the raining bullets. She put her foot on the gas and the tires screeched as she drove wildly out of the parking lot, jumping a curb, causing the car to do a small wheely. Millie slightly peeked up so she could barely see over the steering wheel as the bullets continued to fly nonstop. She finally got far enough where the bullets stop hitting the car and sat up breathing heavily as her heart raced what seemed to be a thousand beats per minute. Millie drove a couple of miles down the road and turned onto a dark side street to gather herself. She made sure no one was tailing her before she pulled over to the side of the road and threw the car into park.

"Fuck you, Seven!" she screamed loudly as if he could hear her cry from where he was. She hit her wheel repeatedly, taking out all of her frustrations. Millie knew that she would have to come at Seven a different way than she had originally planned. He had too much clout in the street for her to try to pay one of his own to get at him. She would have to lay low and resurface wiser and more strategic. Millie turned the car around and headed toward the freeway. She was on her way back home, to her original home . . . Baltimore, Maryland.

Chapter Twenty-six

Three Years Later

Millie looked around the room and watched as the two young females cut the heroin and packaged it up, while wearing doctors masks.

"You are cutting that pack too much," Millie said as she stood over the shoulder of one of the girls sitting at the table. She noticed that she was putting too much lactose on the dope, making it less potent. "That's a sure way to lose customers. Putting out stepped on dope ain't good business," Millie taught, thinking about the days when she used to shoot dope and when she would get a weak pack. She knew how it felt to get stuck with subpar product and that reason alone used to make her go to the opposite side of the town. She was speaking from experience, but the girls would have never known.

They were cramped up in a small apartment in lower east side Baltimore. Millie was counting the money and placing it in a duffle bag, preparing it for Lovie. Lovie was a seventeen-year-old who worked as a mule for Millian. She traveled back and forth from Newark and Canada, transporting dope for Millie. Millie had been back home in Baltimore for three years and within that time she got clean, used Apple's money and connect to get back in the dope game, and became Millie of old: the hustler. Millie once was a part of a crew that reigned supreme in Baltimore, but when death and treachery among the crew entered, their reign ended and Millie moved to Flint. Now Millie was back in her comfort zone and making money; reestablishing her street credibility through Baltimore's black market.

"You ready, li'l mama?" Millie asked as a cigarette hung from the right side of her mouth. Millie had picked up some weight, roughly fifteen pounds. However, it looked good on her. Millie stood up and walked to the table where the two girls where sitting and repeated herself.

"Ready?" Millie asked again.

"Yeah, I'm ready," Lovie said as she pulled down the mask and sat back in her chair as if she was tired. She had been cutting dope for four hours straight and she was mentally exhausted, having to focus on one thing for so long. Millie emphasized that every pack had to be cut just right, so it required precision. Lovie was brown-skinned with a thick frame. She had been a product of the streets and daughter of a drug addict. She could relate to street life and when Millie found her tricking by her apartment, she quickly took her under her wing.

"Cool, here is your bus ticket and a Russian female with a red flower in her hair is going to pick you up. She will tell you what to do when you get there," Millie instructed.

"I know, Millie. You give me this speech every single time," Lovie said in an exasperated tone.

"Yeah, yeah. Well, I'm going to tell yo' ass every time so you can't say you didn't know. Because if anything goes wrong . . . that's your ass," Millie said with a smile, but was as serious as a heart attack and Lovie knew that. Millie handed her the bag and walked to the window, looking down at the project's playground where her workers were stationed slanging product. There wasn't a day that went by that Millie didn't think about killing Seven, but she knew that to catch a wolf, she had to become a wolf. She would have to get on Seven's level to even come close to him and that's exactly what she did. Millie was getting rich off the same thing that she once was a slave to: dope. A knock on the apartment's door sounded throughout the apartment and Millie quickly walked to the door and grabbed the pistol that sat on the stand near the entrance. She stood on her tiptoes and peeked through the hole and quickly put the gun down when she saw who it was. It was Baby, a young hustler who worked under Millie. Baby was her street captain and designated killer. Millie opened the door and Baby stepped in with a brown paper bag in his hand. He handed it to Millie and then kissed her on the cheek.

"Sup, Millie," he said as he entered the room.

"Hey, Baby," Millie answered. Baby was about six foot, brown-skinned, and had a slim build. He wore a long beard and small glasses that gave him an intellectual look rather than a killer. Baby grew up hearing stories about how the infamous street legend Tical had a female "right-hand man" who was one of the best hustlers Baltimore had ever seen. So when Millie came back to Baltimore, it was nothing for her to recruit a team and get respect. Baby had loyalty toward Millie because of his deceased older brother, who Millie used to run with, whose name was Gunplay.

Baltimore's underworld never knew Millie to be a junkie, only a certified hustler. Once Millie got to Baltimore she went cold turkey and never touched a drug since. She had been getting rich with her connect, Hassan.

"Yo', I got the drop on the nigga you wanted me to scope out," Baby said as he sat on the couch. Millie's heart began to speed up as she heard what Baby had said. She instantly knew that he was talking about Seven. Millie couldn't get close to Seven and had been waiting for that particular day for three years.

"Word?" she asked as she looked at him with hopeful eyes.

"Yeah. That nigga is like a ghost though. Nobody really knows where the nigga be at. But, I got the drop on his man. Raheem, Rakim, something like that," Baby said, trying to remember his name.

"Rah," Millie corrected him.

"Yeah, that's it," Baby confirmed. "Word is, is that they expanded to Columbus, Ohio and they moving heavy weight. My people in Ohio said that the boy Rah is mad flashy and running the streets crazy right now. I got a plug on a stripper that he deals with. So that's our first link to the kid Seven."

"Great news," Millie said calmly as flashes of Hazel's face appeared before her eyes, causing a big wave of sadness and guilt to overcome her. She had been trying to find Seven the past years and always came up empty. He had gone into seclusion after Apple's death and no one knew how to find him. With the newfound information about Rah, she was one step closer to getting revenge.

Seven sat back in a beach chair, smoking a blunt on his new yacht. He stared at the waves and slowly bobbed his head to Jay-Z's *Reasonable Doubt* that played out of the small stereo that sat near his feet. He remembered when he was younger, Apple would play that disc over and over and it seemed as if it was the soundtrack to his life. Seven had grown a full, wild beard and was only a fraction of what he used to be. However, he had become a street millionaire after his expansion to Columbus, OH. Seven had surpassed the wealthy mark and had reached a status that most doughboys could only dream about. But the loneliness he felt in his heart far exceeded the happiness wealth could ever bring him. At that point he was just moving dope through the city because it was all he knew and he was addicted to flipping money. After Hazel's death and Apple's untimely demise, Seven had to find a way to cope. This was his uncanny therapy. Seven dumped the ashes into the water from the blunt and breathed in the clear air, thinking about how Hassan told him that he would never get a boat. Seven used his cane to stand and smiled, looking around and knowing that his yacht was two times better than his former connect's.

"You still out here?" Rah said as he walked up from the lower deck with two beautiful women in his arms. Seven turned around to see who was talking over the music and then quickly focused back on the water.

"Yeah, just up here thinking, that's all," Seven said as he took a deep pull of the blunt and blew out smoke circles. Rah took turns tongue kissing the girls on his arms and then headed back down to the lower part of the boat to start round two of the ménage à trois they were partaking in. Little did Rah know, one of the strippers he was sexing was getting paid by Baby to suck all of the info she could about Seven out of him.

Millie pulled into a Holiday Inn right outside of Columbus, OH in a small town called Sandusky. She was in a tinted Yukon truck with five of her most treacherous goons from B-more with her. She was on a mission to give Seven a surprise. Baby was already in the town. He had been there for a couple of weeks, setting up everything for Millie. Millie hopped out of the van. Lovie was driving and ready for whatever also. Millie had been molding Lovie to be just as clever and witty as she was, minus the flaws. The goons hopped out, rocking full beards and two of them wearing religious coofies. They went to room 20 B, using the outside entrance, and waiting for them in the room was Baby and the same stripper that Rah had been with the previous night.

"Sup, Millie," Baby said as he stood from the coffee table that he was sitting at with the stripper.

"Hey, Baby," Millie said he walked over to her and pecked her on the cheek.

"This is her?" Millie asked as she stared at the young red-bone girl who sat at the table looking nervous. Baby nodded his head and Millie immediately went over to her and sat across from her, sensing the girl's discomfort. "Hey, honey," Millie said, greeting the girl with a warm smile. Millie set her purse on the table and opened it, grabbing one of her cigarettes out of the pack and lighting it.

"Hi," the girl said, feeling more comfortable with Millie rather than Baby.

"Look, I know you nervous but you don't have anything to be nervous about, ok?" Millie said as she sat back and puffed the cigarette, blowing it out of the side of her mouth and away from the girl.

"So, you know Rah?" Millie asked, making sure that very thing was everything. The young girl nodded her head as she glanced at the goons that were mugging her from the corner of the hotel room. The girl began to grow antsy and almost reconsidered giving up the information to Millie, but then she thought about the $10,000 that was offered to her by Baby. "I'm getting paid first, right?" the girl said with fear evident in her voice.

Millie immediately signaled for one of her goons to pay the girl and almost immediately the girl had a brown paper bag tossed in front of her on the table. The bag contained all one hundred dollar bills, equaling ten thousand dollars. The girl thumbed through the money and then smiled, feeling much better about what she was about to do. Millie smiled when she saw the look in the girl's eye as she flipped through the money. It was the look of greed and Millie knew that she was one step closer to Seven.

At the end of their conversation, Millie knew were Rah lived, were his main block was, and his tendencies. The girl knew nothing about Seven. The only things she could tell Millie were that Seven was

Rah's boss, he kept a low profile, that Seven loved to boat, and the loading dock that he used. Millie wasn't satisfied with the information, but she was grateful and was going to work with what she had. Millie left the stripper in the room with bag full of cash and a bullet in the head to cover her own tracks. She didn't want anything stopping her from getting to Seven. The possibility of the stripper confessing to Rah about what she had done was too risky for Millie, so she made the executive decision to have one of her goons hit her from point-blank range after she squeezed all of the info she could out of her. Some might call it coldblooded, but Millie called it playing the game the right way.

Baby pulled the bandana that was tied around his neck up and over the lower portion of his face to conceal his identity. Lovie drove while the rest of the goons followed suit and pulled ski masks on their faces while gripping their automatic assault rifles. The tinted van had a sliding door and they all waited patiently until Lovie pulled up to the block so they could light it up. The car was quiet and calm, everyone focusing on the task at hand. Lovie pulled to the start of the block and Baby slowly slid the sliding door open that was on the side of the van. He looked at Lovie and nodded at her, giving her the signal, and she then put the pedal to the metal and the sound of screeching tires filled the air and caught all of the hustlers off guard. Baby flung the door open and bullets began to fly, hitting any and everybody on the block hustling. Millie had ordered this drive-by, not to kill people, but to send a message. Baby let his gun off, catching at least four hustlers in the legs and thighs as he aimed low. The other goons shot in the air, giving everyone a scare. Just like that, ten seconds, they were peeling off the block and gone. Lovie maneuvered the van off the street and they headed back to the low-key hotel that the whole crew was staying at and also where Millie was waiting.

Chapter Twenty-seven

Dopefiends lined up as if they were young kids in a cafeteria line outside the abandoned building as the corner boys prepared to open up shop. The hustlers were posted on a stoop prepared for distribution. Rah had already paid off the cops that patrolled the area, so police never were a problem. It was a flawless operation going on. It was 6:30 a.m. and the first waves of users were trying to get their fix. This group usually consisted of the working class: teachers, city workers, functioning addicts, etc. All from different walks of life, but they all had one thing in common: they were trying to get that monkey off of their backs so they could function right throughout the day.

Rah and one of his street lieutenants sat in a tinted Lexus just a block down from the abandoned building, as he did frequently, and observed the spot make money. However, this time he had an AK-47 in the backseat, ready for whatever should come his way. He had just hit his young boys with the product and within minutes the line was moving. Rah just wanted to make sure that there weren't any of the out-of-towners on the block trying to invade their territory. After he learned about the people from Baltimore coming through and wetting the block up, he had been checking in on it more often, willing to defend his territory. Rah smiled and pulled off, on his way to meet Seven for their daily breakfast together.

"If y'all don't get in line, nobody is getting shit!" one of the young hustlers yelled as he got tired of random fiends cutting in line, trying to get closer to the prize. He saw a bunch of new faces and obviously they weren't hip to the rules, so he had to show some muscle. "Get in line!" he yelled as if they were kids. He saw a male bum steady trying to cut in line and becoming dis-gruntled, disregarding what he had told them. The young hustler got frustrated and walked over to the man who had raggedy clothes on and a long, wild beard.

"Didn't you hear what the fuck I said?" the hustler said as he grabbed the man's arm vio-lently, turning him around. As he made the man face him, he got a big surprise. The bum was not actually a bum, it was Baby. Baby held a chrome

.45 in his hand and shoved it into the gut of the young hustler.

"Surprise, mufucka," Baby said as he unleashed a small smirk. One of the other hustlers on the stoop saw Baby pull out the gun and he slowly went into his hoodie to grab his pistol, but the cold steel of a nine millimeter had just been pressed against his temple.

"Uh-uh. Hold up, don't even think about it," Lovie said as she smiled at him while pressing the steel to his head. She was at the front of the line posing as a fiend also. On cue, Millie's other goons pulled out their strap. When they flashed their guns, everyone scattered, causing total chaos. Millie's squad had been watching the hustlers operate for days, so they knew who was on Seven's team.

After the block had cleared there were only Seven's workers left and all of them hand guns in their faces, totally taken off guard. Millie's crew relieved them of all their own guns, while still having them at gunpoint.

Baby was the first to speak. "Look, li'l niggas. We ain't come to kill you," he said as he tucked his own gun away, showing that he wasn't trying to come on no beef. "My boss wants to give y'all a golden opportunity."

"What you mean?" the hustler said bravely as he had both of his hands up, still not sure if he could trust Baby. He did not fully understand what Baby was getting at.

"Money, of course. I want to give you a choice. You have two options. You can get money with us . . . or not get money at all. If you don't want to get down with our program, we will be at y'all every day until we feel like doing otherwise." Baby unleashed a small grin and stepped back in a non-threatening position. He then continued.

"It is obvious that Seven doesn't give a fuck about his team because we just ran up on y'all without any problems. If y'all fucked with us, shit like this would never happen," Baby said as he looked around at the young hustlers being held at gunpoint by his crew. He continued, "You niggas can be touched . . . but where is Seven? He's untouchable, but what about his crew?" Baby asked rhetorically as he threw his hands up and looked around. There was a brief moment of silence. Obviously what Baby was saying was making a lot of sense to the hustlers. Baby snapped his fingers and instantly his crew put down their guns. Baby grabbed the kid he was standing by. From watching him for the past week, he knew that he was the leader of the block. Baby gave him a wad of cash and a card with a number on it.

"If you trying to get down with the winning team, call," he said just before he faded into the alley along with his crew. Baby left the young hustlers on the corner confused and thinking hard about what he had just proposed. The leader of the block looked at the stack of money in his hands and couldn't believe it. It would have taken him a whole month worth of trapping to stack the amount he had in his hands.

Although Millie wasn't there, she had put the whole plan together and was waiting on Seven's goons to jump ship and come to her side. She knew that by taking over Seven's block, he would eventually come out of seclusion.

Seven sat across from Rah at the table and slid a piece of bacon into his mouth as he stared at the local newspaper. Rah briefly stared at Seven and smirked. Rah still couldn't get used to Seven eating meat. But that was one of the many changes Seven made after he had gotten shot years back. Rah focused on his plate and then felt his phone vibrate on his hip. He immediately answered it, snatching the phone off of his clip and putting it to his ear.

"Yo'," Rah answered. He paused for a minute and then his face frowned up, which caught Seven's attention.

"What the fuck happened?" Rah yelled into the phone and paused. "And they didn't take anything?" Rah questioned. "Okay, just hold tight, I'm on my way."

"What was all of that about?" Seven asked as he sat back and took a deep breath.

"I think them mufuckas from Baltimore is going to be a bigger problem than we thought. They just ambushed the block, but check this out: they didn't take anything. Didn't rob the li'l niggas or nothing. Li'l man said they were asking for you," Rah said, his tone getting lower with each word.

"Asking for me? How do they even know about me, son?" Seven asked, knowing that in the new city of Columbus he had kept a very low profile.

"Don't know," Rah answered, shaking his head from side to side.

Seven wiped his hand with a napkin and tossed it on the table. "Let's go," Seven said as he grabbed his cane that leaned against the table, and stood up. He also grabbed the shoulder harness and put it on. The harness contained two desert eagles, locked and loaded. He then slid his leather coat on and they both headed toward the exit. Seven stopped at his front door and began to unlock the six deadbolt locks he had on the door. Paranoia was a daily part of Seven's personality and Rah wanted to ask him why was he so wary, being that Seven lived in a low-key suburban area and no one knew where he lived except him.

However, Rah remained silent, knowing that he could never truly understand what Seven's mind state was like after he had been almost gunned to death. After a sequence of "click-clacks," all of the locks were unlocked and Seven opened the door, but not before he turned off his security system so he wouldn't trigger it. Seven then glanced at the monitor that was positioned to view his parking garage and cars to check to see if the coast was clear. Once Seven stared at the screen for a few seconds and was satisfied, they exited on their way to the block to see what was going on.

Rah and Seven pulled onto the block, riding in Seven's bulletproof Benz. Rah was driving and he pulled up to the curb where their crew was waiting. All of them were waiting anxiously for their boss to arrive. Seven's passenger-side window rolled down and all eyes were on him. Seven checked his rearview mirror to see if anyone was behind him and then scoped the block. Once he felt safe he looked at the group of hustlers on the stoop. He looked at the leader of the block and also the same hustler who Baby had given the money and card to.

"Get in," Seven said in almost a whisper, but everyone was so quiet and hanging off his every word, that he was heard loud and clear.

Moments later the hustler hopped in the backseat and Rah pulled off of the block. The youngster sat in the backseat feeling butterflies in his stomach. Just the presence of Seven made him nervous. Although he had worked for Seven, he never once met him in person. He always dealt with Rah and no one else.

"What happened?" Rah said as he circled the neighborhood.

"Those same niggas from B-more ran up on us again. They caught us slipping and put the bangers to our head," he explained.

"They hit the stash?" Rah asked.

"Nah, it wasn't even like that. They didn't even come on no robbing shit. He just wanted to talk."

"Talk?" Seven interrupted as he put a blunt in between his lips.

"Yeah. He was talking like he wanted to take over the spot and was saying how his boss could make it worth our while," the young hustler explained, purposely leaving out that Baby had hit him with a stack of money.

"Is that right?" Seven asked as he lit his blunt. "Niggas must think it's a game. Do they know who the fuck I am?" Seven asked as he slowly nodded his head, knowing that he would have to show those B-more cats how he got down.

"So, what you want me to do?" the young hustler asked.

"Get out there and hustle. Stay strapped and don't let niggas run up on you again," Seven said nonchalantly. "Have a nice day, sir," Seven said while puffing on his blunt. The young hustler stepped out of the car and by the way Seven was treating him, the offer that Baby had presented to him and his crew was looking more tempting by the second. He slammed the door and then took a couple of steps back. "Yo', Seven," he called and looked at the tinted window on the passenger side where Seven was sitting. Seconds later Seven rolled down his window while still looking forward and blowing out a thick cloud of smoke. Seven didn't even give him the respect of looking in his direction.

"Yeah?" Seven answered.

"Why you never on the block?" the young hustler asked, knowing that the greatest leaders in history were on the field with their troops at the time of combat. Seven smiled and didn't even think the question was worthy of an answer.

Seven understood that he was the boss and didn't have to answer any questions from anyone. Rah slowly pulled off, leaving the young hustler on the sidewalk alone and unanswered. Seven didn't know, but his arrogance had just cost him his most loyal crew. Seven had just lost killers on his team and Millie had just gained some.

Chapter Twenty-eight

Two weeks had passed and neither Seven nor Rah had heard anything else about the B-more crew coming on their most lucrative block. Actually, they heard nothing from their own crew at all. Rah hadn't even gotten a call from them to re-up with heroin, which threw up red flags, because that block ran through numerous bricks per week on average. Rah was on his way to the block to see what the cause was of the sudden drop in production. He had a surprise waiting on him when he pulled onto the block. He pulled up to the street with a duffle bag full of bricks in his passenger side, ready to hit the youngsters off with the dope even though they hadn't requested a re-up.

Rah stepped out of the car and noticed the group of hustlers sitting on the stoop as usual, but an unfamiliar face was in the middle talking with the hustlers, as fiends loomed around the area like zombies.

"Yo', what the fuck is going on? Why y'all niggas just sitting around?" Rah said in an authoritative tone, knowing that they should have been at their post moving that work.

"Because, it's a new sheriff in town," a man said as he stood up and stepped off the stoop.

"Who the fuck is this nigga?" Rah said, pointing and not even looking at the man, but looking past him. Rah brushed past him, bumping him hard, turning the man's body violently. Rah looked at his crew and the lead young hustler stepped out and put his hand on his waist as if he was going for his gun.

"Handle that nigga," Rah instructed as he continued to walk toward the dope house so he could break down the bricks and distribute them. However, just before Rah reached the door the young hustler spoke. "No, Rah. Why don't you handle him!" the young hustler yelled in a menacing tone, remembering how Rah and Seven belittled him weeks ago.

"What?" Rah said, not believing what he had just heard from the youngster. Rah dropped the bag and knew that his gangster was getting tested, so he was about to show them that he wasn't against putting in work. He pulled out a snub nose pistol and walked hurriedly to the man who had originally stepped out of line, who was Baby.

Rah swiftly grabbed Baby by the neck and then stuck his gun against Baby's forehead.

"You might not want to do that," Baby said as he smiled even though he was looking down a barrel of Rah's gun.

"What nigga?" Rah said, not understanding how Baby could be so calm in such a compromising position.

"Look around," Baby said as he put both of his hands up. Rah's jaws were clenched tightly as he stared at Baby with a burning desire to kill him. Rah finally looked around and saw five different guns being pointed at him by his own crew.

"Oh, it's like that, huh?" Rah asked, not believing how his crew had all of a sudden turned on him. Rah knew he was outnumbered so he released the grip he had on Baby and stepped back, but still had his gun pointed directly at Baby's head.

"Yeah, it's like that," one of the young hustlers yelled as they fixed their aim on Rah's head.

"My boss wants to make you and your man Seven an offer. You can get money with us or you can get pushed out. It's all on you," Baby said as he smirked casually and showed not an ounce of fear, even though he was being held at gunpoint. "This block is not your block anymore. If you want it back, tell Seven to meet me here. Time is of the essence, playboy. My boss will be here to talk business," Baby said as he walked past Rah, disregarding the fact that he had a gun pointed at him, and stepped onto the stoop and sat down. Rah slowly lowered his gun and nodded his head, conceding defeat. He made sure he looked each young hustler in the eye before he walked back to his car, non-verbally letting them know that he would make them pay for their betrayal. Rah knew that the dope game was a big business and he would have to handle it as just that and make plans to see Baby's boss. He grabbed his duffle bag and returned to his car and headed over to see Seven. This was the beginning of a war.

Seven slammed his fist on the table after hearing the news from Rah. He grabbed his cane that leaned against the oak table and slowly stood up. He limped from around his desk in his home office as Rah sat on the leather couch a few feet away from him with his hands folded into one another, shaking his head from side to side.

"Who are these B-more niggas?" Seven questioned as he hobbled to the bar to pour himself a drink.

"Don't know. He just said his boss wanted to meet you tomorrow at noon on the block," Rah said, relaying the message.

"Who is his boss? The nigga got to have some balls. Coming on my block like that?" Seven said as he downed the shot of cognac. "I'ma show his ass! Set up a meeting," Seven said just before he exited the room, leaving Rah there alone. Rah stood up and headed back to the block, so he could set something up between the two bosses: Seven and the unknown second party . . . Millie.

An hour later Rah was pulling back onto the block. A dark blue, luxury Maybach with temporary plates was parked on the block and he pulled up just behind it. He walked up to the stoop where Baby was sitting with a mean mug, and he addressed him.

"Yo', where is your boss?" Rah asked.

"Don't worry about us. Where is Seven?" Baby asked as he leaned back on both of his elbows.

"Take me to your boss, you bitch-ass nigga. Why am I even talking to you right now? I'm speaking on Seven's behalf for now," Rah demanded as waved his hand at Baby, dismissing him as if he was a flunky.

"Okay, have it your way. Boss is in the backseat waiting for you," Baby said as he pointed at the tinted Maybach. Rah immediately looked behind him and spotted the car. Rah, without fear, walked over to the car, and the passenger-side window rolled down. A female's face emerged; it was Lovie.

"Get in the back," she ordered in her heavy Baltimore accent just before rolling the window back up and disappearing again. Rah took a deep breath, patted his waist to make sure his strap was there, and opened the back door. He slid in and what he saw totally surprised him. Millie was sitting in the backseat with her legs crossed, smoking a cigarette.

"Damn, Rah, you look like you just seen a ghost," Millie said as she smiled and looked over at Rah.

"What the fuck?' Rah whispered as he tried to figure out in his head what was going on. But before anything else could be said, Millie swiftly pointed a gun to his head that was concealed on the side of her. The goon in the driver seat along with Lovie also turned around and pointed guns in Rah's face. He was totally vulnerable and taken off guard. He had three locked and loaded weapons pointed at his head, and what he thought was going to be a negotiation turned out to be a plotted-out ambush. Millie reached into Rah's waist and relieved him of his pistol.

"Let's go," she said and her goon turned around and pulled off as she and Lovie still kept their guns on Rah. Millie had already had a plan B if Seven didn't come, and they were doing just that.

The next day Seven rode through the block looking for Rah.

After Rah had left him to meet the B-more crew, he never returned, which had Seven kind of worried.

"Where is this nigga at?" Seven whispered to himself as he scanned the block, cruising slowly down the street in an F-150 truck, his most low-key car. Seven had some of his goons who came with him from Flint tailing him just to have his back if anything popped off. Seven checked his rearview mirror and saw the green Grand Prix that was full of his shooters as he bent the corner. He pulled up on the same block where Rah had been earlier and saw young hustlers posted on each block, obviously hustling. He pulled up on one of them and the young hustler squinted his eyes, trying to see through Seven's light tint. The naïve hustler assumed that Seven was a fiend who was pulling up to get served.

"Yo', I got that *Lady Luck*!" the young hustler said and it instantly made Seven frown his face up.

"*Lady Luck*?" Seven whispered as he stopped and looked at the hustler approaching him. As the young hustler walked up on the car, he looked up and down the street to check for cops. Seven immediately began to think about his hometown, Flint, MI, where *Lady Luck* was a hot commodity and this made him think about Hassan. The boy walked up to the car and Seven rolled down the window. The boy opened his hand, revealing the pack of dope that had the blue stamp that Seven once flooded the streets with.

Is Hassan the one moving in on me? How did he know I know I was in Ohio? Seven thought as so many different things ran through his mind as he caught a glimpse of the stamp on the pack the young hustler had. Seven's face wasn't familiar with the hustler, so he didn't realize that he was trying to serve his former boss. Seven took out twenty dollars and traded the boy for the pack; just to see if what he was thinking was true. He looked at the pack and verified that it was an official *Lady Luck* stamp. He rolled up his window and drove off. "What the fuck is going on?" Seven whispered as he began to drive off; his paranoia had just elevated to an all-time high. Just before he reached the corner, the young hustler who he had belittled weeks ago waved down the car, noticing the truck because Rah occasionally drove it through the hood.

"Yo', have you seen Rah?" Seven asked after he came to a complete stop and rolled down his window.

"Yeah, I seen him," the hustler answered while smirking.

"And? Where the nigga at?" Seven yelled, getting frustrated with the lack of information. All of a sudden the young hustler reached into his pocket and pulled out a small, red box that had a silver bow on it. It was the size of a ring box and he dropped it in Seven's lap. The young hustler turned and walked away from the car. "What the fuck is this?" Seven asked as he frowned up. "Yo'!" Seven yelled as the hustler continued to the stoop where the other hustlers waited for him. Seven picked up the box and examined it. A small tag hung from the bow and he slowly opened it, only to find a number and a few words on it that read: COME TO MAMA He didn't understand the message, but he soon would. Seven then opened it up and what he saw made his heart jump up in his throat. A bloody, severed finger was placed in the box, propped up as if it were an expensive jewelry display, and the putrid smell of decaying human flesh almost made him gag. A diamond, invisible-set pinky ring was placed on the finger and he automatically knew that it was Rah's body part. Seven had bought Rah the ring when they first relocated to Columbus, Ohio as a token of his appreciation for Rah's loyalty. Before Seven could even get angry and ask the young hustler where this came from, bullets began to rain. Seven heard bullets whiz past his head and the thumping noises of the bullets hitting the side of his truck sounded like a black college band on game day. Seven quickly rolled up his window, knowing they were bulletproof, and by instinct he ducked down. He looked and saw that the same young hustlers who used to work for him were now emptying their whole clip at him, trying to murder him. He quickly pulled off the block and his goons who were behind him traded shots with the young boys. The sounds of automatic assault rifles filled the air and the block was on fire; total chaos.

Chapter Twenty-nine

Millie stared out of the window, characteristically puffing on a cigarette with a smug look on her face. She was in deep thought and was alone in the spacious hotel room. Well, she did have one more person in the room with her, but he was soon to be dead. She ordered Baby and her crew to leave her alone with Rah so she could "catch up on old times." Rah squirmed as his body was tightly duct taped to a wooden chair. Blood leaked from his left pinky and dripped onto the Berber carpet as he tried to call Millie a bitch, but couldn't because of the sock stuffed deep down his throat.

"I know what you're probably thinking. How did this dopefiend bitch catch me slipping, right?" Millie asked rhetorically as she left the window and slowly began to circle Rah, watching him as a lioness would her prey. Millie stopped directly in front of him and looked directly into his eyes. She pulled out the sock that was stuffed down his throat and Rah immediately began to cough violently.

"Where do that nigga stay? Tell me or it's *on to the next one!*" Millie joked as she repeated a rap lyric, totally having fun tormenting Rah, threatening to cut off the next finger. She pulled out the sharp pliers that she used to cut off his pinky a day before and waved them around, giving him one last chance to spill the beans before she played doctor and made a surgical cut. "Now, are you sure you ain't trying to come up off that info on your man?" Millie asked.

"Fuck you!" Rah yelled as he tried to break free from the chair, but it was to no avail because Baby had done a number on him. Baby made sure that Rah could never escape the situation on his own.

"You crazy bitch," Rah said as he breathed heavily and began to feel lightheaded because of all the blood he had lost. Millie smiled and shrugged her shoulders.

"Suit yourself," she said as she pulled out a cigarette and put a flame to it. She let it dangle from the left side of her mouth as she took a long pull and knelt down, casually grabbing Rah's finger. "Oh, I almost forgot," Millie said just before she grabbed the sock and forced it down Rah's throat as he tried to turn his head away from her, but she managed to stuff it even further than before.

"Don't want the neighbors to hear, feel me?" Millie asked and she grabbed Rah's middle finger and placed it in between the pliers and looked up at him. "Give that nigga info up. I'm only going to ask you one more time." Although Rah couldn't speak, he wanted to express how he felt. He just barely raised his middle finger slightly as his hands were duct taped together, flipping her off as a smile formed on his face. Without hesitation, Millie squeezed the pliers as hard as she could. The sound of his finger's bone cracking filled the air along with muffled screams and vigorous twitching and jerking. Millie yanked the pliers, trying to rip his finger off, and blood squirted six feet into the air. She yanked for a third time, squeezing even harder, causing his severed finger to fly across the room. Millie had gone mad; mad with revenge and hatred in her heart.

"You want to tell me now, homeboy?" Millie said calmly as she wiped the blood off her face and tossed the pliers onto the bed. She pulled the sock out of his mouth and waited for him to respond. Rah panted heavily as he sweated profusely. Only whimpers could escape his mouth as he began to drool on himself. He was in excruciating pain and began to black out because of the overwhelming pain. His head became heavy and he felt himself slipping out of consciousness.

"Seven is going to kill you, bitch," he managed to whisper with pride just before he fainted and his chin hit his chest. Millie had to admit, she admired his courage but she also knew that she couldn't let Rah die. At least, not at that moment; she still needed him. He was her only connection to Seven and that was who she wanted badly. She smacked the hell out of him and screamed his name, trying to wake him up.

Smack!

"Rah! Don't die on me, you son of a bitch," she yelled as she grabbed him by his jaws and raised his head up. Millie saw that Rah's eyes began to roll in the back of his head and she smacked her lips as she let his head drop back down to his chest. Obviously, her plan to squeeze the information out of Rah wasn't working so she decided to go with her plan B. Rah had a little secret back home. When Baby went through Rah's phone, he discovered baby pictures and text messages from a woman from Flint; Toya, to be exact. It just so happened that Rah was a new father. Millie anticipated Rah's stubbornness and loyalty, that's why she had already sent Baby and half of the crew to Flint to snatch up Toya and the baby for collateral. One way or another, Millie knew Rah was going to give up some info.

Just as Millie picked up her phone to call Baby, a blocked number was incoming and she smiled as she picked up the phone.

"Speak," she said as she held the phone to her ear.

"Yo, who the fuck is this?" Seven said coldly into the phone.

"Hold up. Is that any way to talk to a lady?" Millie said sarcastically as she put her cigarette out on Rah's forehead and began to slowly pace the room.

"Bitch! Fuck you. Put your boss on the phone or whoever sent me this package."

"Seven, relax. You don't remember me, honey?" Millie asked in a sweet voice, but was steadily getting heated by the second.

"What?" Seven asked, not understanding.

"Let me help you out. You tried to have me killed, but instead you . . ." Millie paused as she felt her eyes begin to water just at the thought of Hazel's painful death. She then clenched her jaws and shook the feeling off. "But instead you killed an innocent young lady for no good reason."

The words were like darts to Seven's heart, being that he still had a heavy heart for what he had done to Hazel. He knew exactly who he was talking to. But never in a million years would he had thought that a dopefiend could get to him like Millie had just done. The phone was silent and the sound of Seven inhaling deeply was the only noise.

"Where the fuck is Rah?" Seven asked, quickly getting to the task at hand.

"We are about to play a little game. It's called . . . if you do not come to me, Rah is going to die a horrible death," Millie said, indirectly getting straight to the point.

The sound of Seven laughing filled the phone's speakers. He already knew at that point Rah was going to die. But he also knew that Rah was one of the realest men he had the privilege of knowing and would never tell Millie about his whereabouts. Seven had positioned himself to never get caught slipping and Rah was the only link to him for an enemy to explore.

"Do you know who the fuck I am, Millie? Huh?" Seven said through his clenched teeth. "You can never touch me, believe that! I can touch you, though. That's a promise. So you do me a favor. Tell my nigga, Rah, I love him to death and real niggas do real things!" With that,

Seven hung up the phone, leaving Millie with a dial tone. Millie couldn't believe what Seven had just done. Although Millie had Rah tied up, Seven was still in complete control. Millie threw her phone on the bed and in complete anger she punched Rah square in his nose to take out her frustrations. He was still unconscious, so he didn't feel it, but Millie did as she shook her hand in pain. She had punched him so hard that she broke his nose and also her pointer finger. Millie knew that she would take it to extreme measures to get to Seven and she was willing to go as far as she had to avenge Hazel's death. She was about to get to Seven one way or another. But in the meantime, she was about to cut his legs from under him by taking over his blocks. *Lady Luck* was about to fill the streets of Columbus, Ohio and she knew that a hustler's worst nightmare was a decline in business.

Chapter Thirty

"Wake up!" Baby said as he threw a bucket of ice-cold water onto Rah. Rah had been out for almost a whole day. He slowly raised his head and it took a few seconds for him to regain his focus and remember where he was. He looked up at Baby who had a slight smirk on his face and was looking down at him.

"Got a surprise for you," Baby said as he looked back at Millie. Rah's eyes focused on Millie and he saw Millie cradling an infant in her arms and rocking slowly while looking down at the child. Rah got a glimpse of the baby's face and knew immediately that it was his newborn son.

"If you touch him, I'll—" Rah screamed as his heart dropped to the floor.

"Shhhh!" Millie said as she looked at Rah, while continuing to rock the baby. "You don't want to wake the baby," Millie whispered as she smiled, knowing that she had won the battle. When she saw the pained look in Rah's eyes, she knew that she would get the information she needed to kill Seven.

"Just let him go! He has nothing to do with this," Rah pleaded.

"He has everything to do with this. Now, you have a choice. You can come up off that information or you can kiss your son good-bye. I'll send his ass right where I already sent your baby's mother," Millie said, insinuating that she had killed Toya. Actually, Millie didn't kill Toya, who was tied up in the next room over. Millie didn't want to kill innocent bystanders, just wanted to use them as collateral. By the looks of things, her plan had worked like a charm because Rah instantly broke down in tears at the sound of Toya being dead.

"Okay, okay," Rah whispered as he dropped his head in shame.

"What?" Millie said as her face lit up.

"I said okay! I'll do it. I'll tell you. Just let my son go!" he pleaded as he let the tears flow, but never whimpered. Millie quickly handed the infant over to Baby and got on her knees, directly in front of Rah. She grabbed him harshly by his jaws and pressed the issue.

"Where is he?" she asked as she felt her adrenaline began to pump.

"3702 Vanderbilt Way. It's in a small suburb called Sudbury, right outside of Columbus," Rah admitted. He dropped his head and shook it in shame, hating that he had just told them about Seven's safe haven. "He has security and cameras everywhere on the property. The only way you can get him is through his parking garage. It's the only place he doesn't have cameras." Millie quickly looked at Lovie who was sitting in the corner of the room and threw her head in the direction of the door, signaling her to check out to see if what Rah said was true.

"It's already evident that I am going to kill you eventually. However, if you're telling the truth, your family will live. But, if you're lying to me . . . I feel sorry for them," Millie said as she stood up and began to put her plan in motion. She grabbed the infant from Baby and walked out, going over to the next room where Toya was tied up, waiting.

Chapter Thirty-one

Three weeks later, Rah's body was found hanging from a telephone pole on the same block that he once controlled. Millie was sending a message and letting people know there was a new regime in Columbus, Ohio. Millie's crew was judge, jury, and executioner and that was unmistakable. With Rah's death, Seven lost a brother and his best friend. Millie kept her word and let Rah's baby live, dropping him at a random hospital, but Toya wasn't so lucky. She was also found dead in a hotel room, while tied to a chair with a single shot to the head. Once Seven got the news, he knew that his empire was crumbling, but what he couldn't understand was how Millie did it. Little did he know, she had one of the most ruthless crews Baltimore had ever seen on her side and Millie's street IQ was equivalent to a scholar's Harvard degree in academics. He had finally met his match, so he went into seclusion after burying Rah properly, along with his baby's mother. Seven's blocks had all been stripped away from him. He had no more territory throughout Columbus. It all seemed to happen so fast. Seven decided to leave all of his dope in the streets and not try to collect on what he had fronted hustlers throughout the city. Millie had the whole city on lock and Seven's paranoia was at an all-time high. He stood at the edge of his yacht smoking a blunt, ready to set sail. He was going to use this time to reflect and regroup.

Millie smiled as she sat back and looked at the small metal remote in her hand that had a red button on it. It was a detonator to the bombs she had placed under Seven's yacht.

Millie had sent her goon to Seven's house a week earlier and put tracking devices on his cars so they could know his whereabouts and set him up perfectly for his demise. Millie watched Seven closely, waiting for the best time to send him to his grave. She wanted his death to be special . . . to be classic. She owed that to her Hazelnut. Millie knew Seven was scheduled to set sail that afternoon and couldn't wait to give him his big surprise. He would never get a chance to leave that dock on that day and Millie was anticipating blowing him up and sending him to his maker. She sat at an Italian restaurant with her crew as they celebrated their win and last day in Ohio. Bottles of the house's most expensive champagne lined up on the table. Millie felt the feeling of sweet victory.

"Ohio was nice, but I'm ready to go back home to B-more," Millie said as she sat at the head of the table. "This is to life," Millie said as she raised her glass.

"To life!" Baby said as he smiled. Baby looked at Millie and placed his hand on top of hers under the table. Millie smiled and felt a tingle go up her back. At that moment, for the first time, she looked at Baby in a different light. She loved him from the bottom of her heart and his loyalty and realness was unmatched. She knew she had a real nigga on her team and she respected it. Everyone at the table downed the drink and the celebration continued for the next hour.

Millie looked outside and the line of luxury cars were being pulled up from the valet so they could leave. She made a couple of her goons stay in Ohio to continue what she had started and they were to be her lieutenants and hold down Ohio while she, Baby, and Lovie were going to return to Baltimore. Millie's drug empire had just expanded, and what she thought was going to be a personal trip to Ohio for revenge ended being a lucrative business trip, too. Perfect!

The waitress brought Millie the bill and placed the bag of her unfinished food at her feet.

"Thanks for coming. Have a nice night," the waitress said just before she turned around and left toward the back. Millie smiled and took the bill as she and Baby remained at the table as everyone prepared to leave. Millie left a crisp hundred-dollar bill as a tip for the nice waitress. Millie was about to head out, but had one more thing to do. She looked at the detonator and smiled and so did Baby.

"I have been waiting for this for so long," Millie said as she looked at the device.

"I know. You ready?" Baby asked as he smiled and playfully punched Millie in the arm.

"Yeah," Millie said as she smiled and took a deep breath.

"I'ma let you make that call alone. I'ma pull the car to the front door and will be waiting for you. We got a long drive," Baby said as he stood up and watched the whole crew make their way to the exit. Baby started to leave, but Millie stopped him.

"Baby!" she said as she looked into his eyes.

"What up, ma?" he asked as he stopped in his tracks and looked back at her.

"I love you," Millie said. But the way she said it, it wasn't a platonic "I love you" and they both sensed that. Baby smiled and his heart began to flutter. He had been waiting on that day for many years if Millie knew it or not.

"I know. I love you too, Millie," he said as he walked up to her and gently cradled the back of her neck. He slowly kissed her soft, full lips and let his tongue slide into hers. Millie felt chills and her love button began to thump at the feel of his lips pressed against hers. With that, Baby left to get the car, leaving Millie sitting there, smiling. Millie took another deep breath and watched him leave. She then picked up her phone to give Seven his big surprise. She picked up her secured phone and called.

Seven stood at the edge of his yacht ready to set sail. He looked back at his newly hired, elderly Spanish maid, who was rocking Rah Jr. to sleep. Seven smiled knowing that Big Rah would have appreciated him taking responsibility for his son. *Real niggas do real things,* lingered in Seven's head; a creed that he and Rah lived and died by.

"Let me see him, Wilma," Seven said as he smiled and opened his arms. She brought the baby to him and Seven grabbed him and kissed him on the forehead.

"I'ma raise you as one of my own, li'l man," Seven whispered as he looked down at the baby, who already had resemblance to his father. Seven stared into the water and gave the deck worker thumbs up, signaling him to lift the anchor so they could set sail. All of a sudden, Seven's phone rang and he looked at the caller ID, which was blocked. He knew exactly who it was.

"Hello," he said as he placed the phone between his ear and shoulder and began to rock the baby.

"You took the only thing that I had good in my life, when you took Hazel. Do you know that?" Millie asked.

"Look, Millie. I never meant to hurt Hazel. That pack was meant for you. Do you know that I think about that girl every single day? She is the first thing on my mind when I wake up and the last thought in my head before I go to sleep. I know I will have to suffer for what I did, but who are you to decide what it is? Huh?" Seven asked, really wanting to tell Millie how he felt about Hazel for once and for all. "That is the only woman who ever captured my heart. The only one! I will always love her!"

"Yeah, but it's too late for all of that. I just wanted to hear your voice before you die. I hope you rot in hell," Millie said as she clenched her jaws so tight, it seemed as if she would crack a tooth.

Seven laughed and continued to rock the baby. "Remember when I told you I was untouchable? Believe that! I ain't new to this, I'm true to this," Seven said.

"See you in hell," Millie said as she stared out of the restaurant's window, looking at her crew smiling and joking while getting into their cars. Millie pushed the red button and waited to hear the thundering sounds of explosives just before she heard a dial tone. The C4 dynamites that Millie's goons placed under Seven's boat were enough to blow him up, three times over. The sounds of explosions went off, but not from Seven's boat . . . from the cars of her crew, including Baby. Millie's heart broke in half as she saw her whole crew go up in flames right before her eyes. Her hands began to shake as she dropped the detonator. She was speechless, frozen in astonishment while watching the flying metal parts and fireballs form from the explosion.

"I see you're not talking as much these days, huh?" Seven said as he thought back to a week earlier, when he watched Millie's goons sneak into his garage and place devices under his cars. He sat back and watched them on his surveillance camera while laughing. All the time Millie thought she was watching Seven, he was watching her. He knew that Rah was aware of how he would closely survey his parking garage and Rah ultimately helped Seven win the battle. Rah knew exactly what he was doing when he gave Millie the info on Seven.

"I told you I was untouchable, bitch. You just killed your whole crew by pushing that button," Seven said smoothly and calmly. Millie dropped to her knees completely shocked at the turn of events. She listened to Seven's words and they were killing her softly.

"If I was you, I would get the hell out of there," Seven said as he started up the yacht's engine and slowly pulled out of the dock. "I want you to look at your feet and into that bag you got right there," Seven suggested.

Millie did as he said and looked into the big paper bag that the waitress had given her. She saw a stack of Styrofoam takeout boxes. Millie then opened one up and saw bricks of dope inside of the boxes. "What the fuck?" she whispered as she couldn't believe her eyes.

"Now I want you to look at the back entrance," Seven said, just before he hung up the phone and continued to sail with a big smile on his face.

Once Millie turned around she saw Feds with labeled bulletproof vests on, rushing into the restaurant with their guns drawn. She dropped the phone and held her head up high. *I'm still a bad bitch,* Millie thought as she fully understood that karma had just come full circle.

"Freeze, bitch! Put your hands up where I can see them!" an officer yelled. Millie had no choice but to grin at Seven's antics. Seven had outwitted her and outplayed her in the chess-like street game.

"Motherfucka!" Millie whispered as she put her hands up and shook her head from side to side. The federal agents rushed her and confiscated ten bricks of raw heroin, which was a guaranteed life sentence. Seven knew he could have killed Millie, but he wanted her to live and suffer, just as he would have to do for the remainder of his life. The game was over and so is the story for now.

ORDER FORM
URBAN BOOKS, LLC
97 N18th Street
Wyandanch, NY 11798

Name (please print):_____

Address:_____

City/State:_____

Zip:_____

QTY	TITLES	PRICE

Shipping and handling: add $3.50 for 1st book, then $1.75 for each additional book.
Please send a check payable to:
Urban Books, LLC
Please allow 4-6 weeks for delivery